Stopping for a Spell

ALSO BY

Diana Wynne Jones

Archer's Goon

Aunt Maria

Believing Is Seeing: *Seven Stories*

Castle in the Air

Dark Lord of Derkholm

Dogsbody

Eight Days of Luke

Fire and Hemlock

Hexwood

Hidden Turnings:
A Collection of Stories Through Time and Space

The Homeward Bounders

Howl's Moving Castle

The Merlin Conspiracy

The Ogre Downstairs

Power of Three

A Tale of Time City

The Time of the Ghost

Warlock at the Wheel and Other Stories

Wild Robert

Witch's Business

Year of the Griffin

Yes, Dear

THE WORLDS OF CHRESTOMANCI

Book 1: Charmed Life

Book 2: The Lives of Christopher Chant

Book 3: The Magicians of Caprona

Book 4: Witch Week

Mixed Magics: *Four Tales of Chrestomanci*

The Chronicles of Chrestomanci, Volume I
(Contains Books 1 and 2)

The Chronicles of Chrestomanci, Volume II
(Contains Books 3 and 4)

THE DALEMARK QUARTET

Book 1: Cart and Cwidder

Book 2: Drowned Ammet

Book 3: The Spellcoats

Book 4: The Crown of Dalemark

Diana Wynne Jones

Stopping for a Spell

Three fantasies

Illustrations by
Mark Zug

Greenwillow Books
An Imprint of HarperCollins*Publishers*

GREENWILLOW BOOKS

CONTENTS

Chair Person   1
1. Auntie Christa's Box   3
2. Something in the Garden Shed   10
3. A Busy Night   20
4. Coffee Morning   27
5. Junk Shop   34
6. Party Games   45

The Four Grannies   57
1. Erg Gets an Idea   59
2. More Grannies Arrive   64
3. Emily Gets Converted   70
4. A Large Yellow Teddy Bear   74
5. How to Keep Four Grannies Busy   79
6. Erg's Invention Works   85
7. Supergranny   91

Who Got Rid of Angus Flint?   99
1. Angus Flint Arrives   101
2. The Smell in the Night   106
3. Roller Skates and Stew   111
4. Cream Teas   117
5. Angus Flint's Revenge   122
6. The Tables Turn   126

Stopping for a Spell

Chair Person

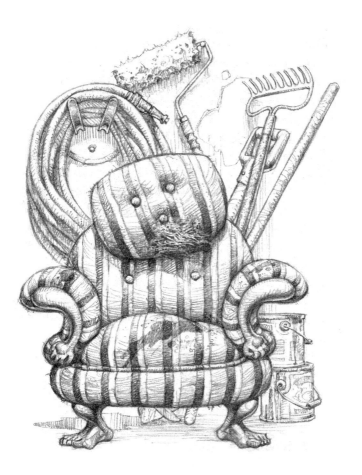

1

Auntie Christa's Box

What happened to the old striped armchair was Auntie Christa's fault.

The old chair had stood in front of the television for as long as Simon and Marcia could remember. As far as they knew, the cushion at the top had always been tipped sideways and it had never been comfortable to sit in. The seat was too short for Dad and too low for Mum and too high for Simon or Marcia. Its arms were the wrong shape for putting things on. Perhaps that was why there was a coffee stain on one arm and a blot of ink on the other. There was a sticky brown patch on the seat where Simon and Marcia had once had a fight for the ketchup bottle. Then, one evening, the sideways cushion at the top wore out. Whatever the chair was stuffed with began to ooze out in a spiky brown bush.

"The armchair's grown a beard," said Simon.

"It looks as if someone's smashed a hedgehog on it," Marcia said.

Dad stood and looked at it. "Let's get rid of it," he said. "I've never liked it, anyway. I tell you what—we can sit the guy in it on Guy Fawkes night. That will make a really good bonfire."

Marcia thought this was a very good idea. Now she thought about it, she had never liked that chair either. The purple and orange and pale blue stripes on it never seemed to go with anything else in the room. Simon was not so sure. He always liked things that he *knew*, and he had known that chair all his life. It seemed a shame to burn it on the bonfire. He was glad when Mum objected.

"Oh, you can't throw it out!" Mum said. "It's got such a personality!"

"But it's worn out," said Dad. "It wasn't new when we bought it. We can afford to buy a much nicer one now."

They argued about it, until Simon began to feel sorry for the old chair and even Marcia felt a little guilty about burning a chair that was old enough to have a personality.

"Couldn't we just sell it?" she asked.

"Don't *you* start!" said Dad. "Even the junk shop wouldn't want a mucky old thing like—"

At that moment Auntie Christa came in. Auntie

Christa was not really an auntie, but she liked everyone to call her that. As usual, she came rushing in through the kitchen, carrying three carrier bags and a cardboard box and calling, "Coo-ee! It's me!" When she arrived in the living room, she sank down into the striped armchair and panted, "I just had to come in. I'm on my way to the Community Hall, but my feet are killing me. I've been all afternoon collecting prizes for the children's party for the Caring Society on Saturday—I must have walked *miles*! But you wouldn't *believe* what *wonderful* prizes people have given me. Just look." She dumped her cardboard box on the arm of the chair—it was the arm with the ink blot—in order to fetch a bright green teddy bear out of one of the carrier bags. She wagged the teddy in their faces. "Isn't he *charming*?"

"So-so," said Dad, and Marcia added, "Perhaps he'd look better without the pink ribbon." Simon and Mum were too polite to say anything.

"And here's such a lovely clockwork train!" Auntie Christa said, plunging the teddy back in the bag and pulling out a broken engine. "Isn't it exciting? I can't stay long enough to show you everything—I have to go and see to the music for the Senior Citizens' Dance in a minute— but I think I've just got time to drink a cup of tea."

"Of course," Mum said guiltily. "Coming up." She dashed into the kitchen.

Auntie Christa was good at getting people to do things. She was a very busy lady. Whatever went on at the Community Hall—whether it was Youth Club Disco, Children's Fancy Dress, Mothers' Choir, Dog Training, Soup for the Homeless, or a Bring-and-Buy Sale—Auntie Christa was sure to be in the midst of it, telling people what to do. She was usually too busy to listen to what other people said. Mum said Auntie Christa was a wonder, but Dad quite often muttered "Quack-quack-quack" under his breath when Auntie Christa was talking.

"Quack-quack," Dad murmured as Auntie Christa went on fetching things out of her bags and telling them what good prizes they were. Auntie Christa had just got through all the things in the bags and was turning to the cardboard box on the arm of the chair when Mum came dashing back with tea and cookies.

"Tea!" Auntie Christa said. "I can always rely on a cup of tea in this house!"

She turned gladly to take the tea. Behind her the box slid into the chair.

"Never mind," said Auntie Christa. "I'll show you what's in there in a minute. It will thrill Simon and Marcia—oh, that reminds me! The African Aid Coffee Morning has to be moved this Saturday because the Stamp Collectors need the hall. I think we'll have the coffee morning here instead. You can easily manage coffee and cakes for twenty on Saturday, can't you?" she asked Mum. "Marcia and Simon can help you."

"Well—" Mum began, while Dad looked truly dismayed.

"That's settled, then," said Auntie Christa, and quickly went on to talk about other things. Dad and Simon and Marcia looked at one another glumly. They knew they were booked to spend Saturday morning handing around cakes and soothing Mum while she fussed. But it was worse than that.

"Now, you'll never guess what's in the box," Auntie Christa said, cheerily passing her cup for more tea. "Suppose we make it a competition. Let's say that whoever guesses wrong has to come and help me with the Caring Society party on Saturday afternoon."

"I think we'll all be busy—" Dad tried to say.

"No refusing!" Auntie Christa cried. "People are so wicked, the way they always try to get out of doing good deeds! You can have one guess each. And I'll give you a clue. Old Mr. Pennyfeather gave me the box."

As old Mr. Pennyfeather kept the junk shop, there could have been almost anything in the box. They all thought rather hard.

Simon thought the box had rattled as it tipped. "A tea set," he guessed.

Marcia thought she had heard the box slosh. "A goldfish in a bowl," she said.

Mum thought of something that might make a nice

prize and guessed, "Dolls' house furniture."

Dad thought of the sort of things that were usually in Mr. Pennyfeather's shop and said, "Mixed-up jigsaws."

"You're all wrong, of course!" Auntie Christa said while Dad was still speaking. She sprang up and pulled the box back to the arm of the chair. "It's an old-fashioned conjurer's kit. Look. Isn't it thrilling?" She held up a large black top hat with a big shiny blue ball in it. Water—or something—was dripping out of the hat underneath. "Oh, dear," Auntie Christa said. "I think the crystal ball must be leaking. It's made quite a puddle in your chair."

Dark liquid was spreading over the seat of the chair, mixing with the old ketchup stain.

"Are you sure you didn't spill your tea?" Dad asked.

Mum gave him a stern look. "Don't worry," she said. "We were going to throw the chair away anyway. We were just talking about it when you came."

"Oh, good!" Auntie Christa said merrily. She rummaged in the box again. "Look, here's the conjurer's wand," she said, bringing out a short white stick wrapped in a string of little flags. "Let's magic the nasty wet away so that I can sit down again." She tapped the puddle in the chair with the stick. "There!"

"The puddle hasn't gone," said Dad.

"I thought you were going to throw the hideous old thing away anyway," Auntie Christa said crossly. "You should be quite ashamed to invite people for a coffee morning and ask them to sit in a chair like this!"

"Then perhaps," Dad said politely, "you'd like to help us carry the chair outside to the garden shed?"

"I'd love to, of course," Auntie Christa said, hurriedly putting the hat and the stick back into the box and collecting her bags, "but I must dash. I have to speak to the Vicar before I see about the music. I'll see you all at the Caring Society party the day after tomorrow at four-thirty sharp. Don't forget!"

This was a thing Simon and Marcia had often noticed about Auntie Christa. Though she was always busy, it was always other people who did the hard work.

2

Something in the Garden Shed

Now Mum had told Auntie Christa they were going to throw the chair away, she wanted to do it at once.

"We'll go and get another one tomorrow after work," she told Dad. "A nice blue, I think, to go with the curtains. And let's get this one out of the way now. I'm sick of the sight of it."

It took all four of them to carry the chair through the kitchen to the back door, and they knocked most of the kitchen chairs over doing it. For the next half hour they thought they were not going to get it through the back door. It stuck, whichever way they tipped it. Simon was quite upset. It was almost as if the chair was trying to stop them throwing it away. But they got it into the garden in the end. Somehow, as they staggered across the lawn with it, they knocked the top off Mum's new sundial and flattened a rosebush. Then they had to stand it sideways in order to wedge it inside the shed.

"There," Dad said, slamming the shed door and dusting his hands. "That's out of the way until Guy Fawkes Day."

He was wrong, of course.

The next day Simon and Marcia had to collect the key from next door and let themselves into the house, because Mum had gone straight from work to meet Dad and buy a new chair. They felt very gloomy being in the empty house. The living room looked queer with an empty space where the chair had been. And both of them kept remembering that they would have to spend Saturday helping in Auntie Christa's schemes.

"Handing around cakes might be fun," Simon said doubtfully.

"But helping with the party won't be," said Marcia. "We'll have to do all the work. Why couldn't one of us have guessed what was in that box?"

"What *are* Caring Society children, anyway?" asked Simon.

"I *think*," said Marcia, "that they *may* be the ones who have to let themselves into their houses with a key after school."

They looked at one another. "Do you think we

count?" said Simon. "Enough to win a prize, anyway. I wouldn't mind winning that conjuring set. It was a real top hat, even if the crystal ball did leak."

Here they both began to notice a distant thumping noise from somewhere out in the garden. It suddenly felt unsafe being alone in the house.

"It's only next door hanging up pictures again," Marcia said bravely.

But when they went rather timidly to listen at the back door, the noise was definitely coming from the garden shed.

"It's next door's dog got shut in the shed again," Simon said. It was his turn to be brave. Marcia was scared of next door's dog. She hung back while Simon marched over the lawn and tugged and pulled until he got the shed door open.

It was not a dog. There was a person standing inside the shed. The person stood and stared at them with his little head on one side. His little fat arms waved about as if he was not sure what to do with them. He breathed in heavy snorts and gasps as if he was not sure how to breathe.

"Er, hn hm," he said as if he was not sure how to speak either. "I appear to have been shut in your shed."

"Oh—*sorry!*" Simon said, wondering how it had happened.

The person bowed, in a crawlingly humble way. "I—hn hm—am the one who is snuffle sorry," he said. "I have made—hn hm—you come all the way here to let me out." He walked out of the shed, swaying and bowing from foot to foot.

Simon backed away, wondering if the person walked like that because he had no shoes on. He was a solid, plump person with wide, hairy legs. He was wearing a most peculiar striped one-piece suit that only came to his knees.

Marcia backed away behind Simon, staring at the person's stripy arms. He waved them in a feeble way as he walked. There was a blot of ink on one arm and what looked like a coffee stain on the other. Marcia's eyes went to the person's plump striped stomach. As he came out into the light, she could see that the stripes were sky blue, orange, and purple. There was a damp patch down the middle and a dark, sticky place that could have been ketchup, once. Her eyes went up to his sideways face. There was a beard on the person's chin that looked rather as if someone had smashed a hedgehog on it.

"Who *are* you?" she said.

The person stood still. His arms waved like seaweed in a current. "Er, hn hm, I am Chair Person," he said. His sideways face looked pleased and rather smug about it.

Marcia and Simon, of course, both felt awful about it. He was the armchair. They had put him in the shed ready to go on the bonfire. Now he was alive. They hoped very much that Chair Person did not know that they had meant to burn him.

"Won't you come inside?" Simon said politely.

"That is *very* kind of you," Chair Person said, crawlingly humble again. "I—hn hm snuffle—hope that won't be too much trouble."

"Not at all!" they both said heartily.

They went toward the house. Crossing the lawn was quite difficult because Chair Person did not seem to have learned to walk straight yet, and he talked all the time. "I believe I am—hn hm—Chair Person," he said, crashing into what was left of the sundial and knocking it down, "because I think I am. Snuffle. Oh dear, I appear to have destroyed your stone pillar."

"Not to worry," Marcia said kindly. "It was broken last night when we—I mean, it was broken anyway."

"Then—hn hm—as I was saying," Chair Person said, veering the other way, "that this is what snuffle wise men say. A person who thinks is a Person." He cannoned into the apple tree. Most of the apples Dad had meant to pick that weekend came showering and bouncing down onto the grass. "Oh, dear," said Chair Person. "I appear to have loosened your fruit."

"That's all right," Simon and Marcia said politely. But since Chair Person, in spite of seeming so humble, did not seem very sorry about the apples and just went on talking and weaving about, they each took hold of one of his waving arms and guided him to the back door.

"Only the finest snuffle apples," said Chair Person as he bashed into both sides of the back door, "from the finest—hn hm—orchards go into Kaplan's Peasant Pies. This is one of many snuffle facts I know. Er, hm, very few people have watched as much television as I have," he added, knocking over the nearest kitchen chair.

Marcia picked the chair up, thinking of the many, many times she had gone out of the living room and forgotten to turn the television off. Chair Person, when he was an armchair, must have watched hours of commercials and hundreds of films.

Simon turned Chair Person around and sat him in the

kitchen chair. Chair Person went very humble and grateful. "You are—hn hm—treating me with such kindness," he said, "and I am going to cause you a lot of snuffle trouble. I appear to need something to eat. I am not sure what to do about it. Do I—hn hm—eat *you?*"

"We'll find you something to eat," Simon said quickly.

"Eating people is wrong," Marcia explained.

They hurried to find some food. A tin of spaghetti seemed easiest, because they both knew how to do that. Simon opened the tin and Marcia put it in a saucepan with the gas very high to get the spaghetti hot as soon as possible. Both of them cast nervous looks at Chair Person in case he tried to eat one of them. But Chair Person sat where he was, waving his arms gently. "Hn hm, Spiggley's tasty snacks," he said. "Sunshine poured from a tin." When Marcia put the steaming plateful in front of him and Simon laid a spoon and a fork on either side of it, Chair Person went on sitting and staring.

"You can eat it," Simon said kindly.

"Er, hn hm," Chair Person said. "But this is not a complete meal. I shall have to trouble you for a napkin and salt and pepper. And I think people usually snuffle eat by candlelight with soft music in the background."

They hurried to find him the salt, the pepper mill, and a paper towel. Simon fetched the radio and turned it on. It was playing country and western, but Simon turned it down very low and hoped it would do. He felt so sorry for Chair Person that he wanted to please him. Marcia ran upstairs and found the candlesticks from Mum's dressing table and two red candles from last Christmas. She felt so guilty about Chair Person that she wanted to please him as much as Simon did.

Chair Person was very humble and grateful. While he told them how kind they were being, he picked up the pepper mill and began solemnly grinding pepper over the spaghetti. "Er, hn hm, with respect to you two fine kind people," he said as he ground, "eating people is a time-honored custom."

Simon and Marcia quickly got to the other side of the table. But Chair Person only took up the fork and raked the spaghetti into a new heap, and ground more pepper over that. "There were tribes in South snuffle America," he said, "who believed it was quite correct to—hn hm— eat their grandparents. I have a question. Is Spiggley's another word for spaghetti?"

"No," said Marcia. "It's a name."

Chair Person raked the spaghetti into a different-shaped heap and went on grinding pepper over it. "When the snuffle grandparents were dead," he said, "they cooked the grandparents and the whole tribe had a feast."

Marcia remembered seeing something like this on television. "I watched that program, too," she said.

"You—hn hm—will not know this," Chair Person said, raking the spaghetti into another new shape and grinding another cloud of pepper over it. "Only the sons and daughters of the dead men were allowed to eat the brains." This time he spread the spaghetti flat and ground pepper very carefully over every part of it. "This was so that snuffle the wisdom of the dead man could be passed on to his family," he said.

By this time the spaghetti was gray. Simon and Marcia could not take their eyes off it. It must have been hot as fire by then. They kept expecting Chair Person to sneeze, since he seemed to have trouble breathing anyway, but he just went on grinding pepper and explaining about cannibals.

Simon wondered if Chair Person perhaps did not know how to eat. "You're supposed to put the spaghetti in your mouth," he said.

Chair Person held up the pepper mill and shook it. It was empty. So he put it down at last and picked up the spoon. He did seem to know how to eat, but he did it very badly, snuffling and snorting, with ends dangling out of his mouth. Gray juice dripped through his smashed-hedgehog beard and ran down his striped front. But the pepper did not seem to worry him at all. Simon

was thinking that maybe Chair Person did not have taste buds like other people when the back door opened and Mum and Dad came in.

"What happened to the rest of the sundial?" said Mum. "I leave you alone just for—" She saw Chair Person and stared.

"What have you kids done to those apples?" Dad began. Then he saw Chair Person and stared, too.

A Busy Night

Both Simon and Marcia had had a sort of hope that Chair Person would vanish when Mum and Dad came home, or at least turn back into an armchair. But nothing of the sort happened. Chair Person stood up and bowed.

"Er, hn hm," he said. "I am Chair Person. Good snuffle evening."

Mum's eyes darted to the ink blot on Chair Person's waving sleeve, then to the coffee stain, and then on to the damp smear on his front. She turned and dashed away into the garden.

Chair Person's arms waved like someone conducting an orchestra. "I am the one causing you all this trouble with your apples," he said, in his most crawlingly humble way. "You are so kind to—hn hm—forgive me so quickly."

Dad clearly could not think what to say. After gulping a little, he said in a social sort of way, "Staying in the neighborhood, are you?"

Here Mum came dashing back indoors. "The old chair's not in the shed anymore," she said. "Do you think he *might* be—?"

Chair Person turned to her. His arms waved as if he were a conductor expecting Mum to start singing. "Your—hn hm—husband has just made me a very kind offer," he said. "I shall be delighted to stay in this house."

"I—" Dad began.

"Er, hn hm, needless to say snuffle," said Chair Person, "I shall not cause you more trouble than I have to. Nothing more than—hn hm—a good bed and a television set in my room."

"Oh," said Mum. It was clear she could not think what to say either. "Well, er, I see you've had some supper—"

"Er, hn hm, most kind," said Chair Person. "I would love to have some supper as soon as possible. In the meantime, a snuffle flask of wine would be most—hn hm—welcome. I appear to have a raging thirst."

Marcia and Simon were not surprised Chair Person was thirsty after all that pepper. They got him a carton of orange juice and a jug of water before they all hurried away to put a camp bed in Simon's room and make Marcia's bedroom ready for Chair Person. Marcia could see that Mum and Dad both had the same kind of dazed, guilty feelings about Chair Person that she had. Neither of them quite believed he was really their old armchair, but Mum put clean sheets on the bed and Dad carried the television up to Marcia's room. Chair Person seemed to get people that way.

When they came downstairs, the fridge door was open and the table was covered with empty orange juice cartons.

"I—hn hm—appear to have drunk all your orange juice," Chair Person said. "But I would be willing to drink lemon squash instead. I happen snuffle to know that it has added glucose, which puts pep into the poorest parts."

He sat at the table and slurped lemon squash while Marcia helped Mum get supper. Simon went to look for Dad, who was hiding behind a newspaper in the living room. "Did you buy a new armchair?" Simon asked.

"Yes," said Dad. "Hush. That thing in the kitchen might get jealous."

"So you *do* believe he is the armchair!" Simon said.

"I don't *know!*" Dad groaned.

"I think he is," Simon said. "I'm quite sorry for him. It must be hard to suddenly start being a person. I expect he'll learn to speak and breathe and behave like a real person quite soon."

"I hope you're right," said Dad. "If he just learns to stop waving his arms in that spooky way, I shall be quite pleased."

For supper, Chair Person ate five pizzas and six helpings of chips. In between, he waved his arms and explained, "I—hn hm—have a large appetite for my size, though I do not always need to snuffle eat. I am strange that way. Could I trouble you for some Mannings' fruity brown sauce? I appear to have eaten all your ketchup. I think I shall enjoy my—hn hm—life with you here. I suggest that tomorrow we go on—hn hm—a short tour of Wales. I think I should go to snuffle Snowdon and then down a coal mine."

"I'm sorry—" Dad began.

"Er, hn hm, Scotland then," said Chair Person. "Or would you rather charter an aeroplane and take me to France?"

"We can't go anywhere tomorrow," Mum said firmly. "There's Auntie Christa's party in the evening and the coffee morning for African Aid before that."

Chair Person did not seem at all disappointed. He said, "I shall enjoy that. I happen to—hn hm—know a great deal about Africa. At the end of the day it must be snuffle said that not nearly enough is being done to help Africa and the third world. Why, in Kenya alone . . ." And he was talking almost word for word—apart from the snuffles—the way last night's television program on Africa had talked.

Before long Simon and Marcia had both had enough. They tiptoed away to Simon's room and went to bed early.

"I suppose he's here for good," Simon said.

"He hasn't any other home," Marcia said, wriggling her way into the uncomfortable camp bed. "And he *has* lived here for years in a sort of way. Do you think it was the stuff that dripped from the crystal ball that brought him alive? Or Auntie Christa tapping him with the wand? Or both?"

"Perhaps she could look after him," Simon said hopefully. "She does good works. Someone's going to have to teach him all the things that aren't on television."

They could hear Chair Person's voice droning away downstairs. It was a loud voice, with a bleat and a bray to it, like a cow with a bad cold. After an hour or so it was clear that Mum and Dad could not stand any more of it either. Simon and Marcia heard them coming to bed early, too. They heard Chair Person blundering upstairs after them.

"Er, hn hm—oh, dear!" his voice brayed. "I appear to have broken this small table."

After that there was a lot of confused moving about and then the sound of running water. Chair Person's voice bleated out again. "Tell me—er, hn hm—is the water supposed to run all over the bathroom floor?"

They heard Mum hurry to the bathroom and turn the taps off. "There are such a lot of things he doesn't know," Marcia said sleepily.

"He'll learn. He'll be better tomorrow," Simon said.

They went to sleep then. There was the first frost of winter that night. They woke up much earlier than they had hoped because it was so cold. Their blankets somehow seemed far too thin and there was white frost on the inside of the bedroom window. They stared at it, with their teeth chattering.

"I've never seen that before," said Simon.

"It's all feathery. It would be pretty if it wasn't so cold," said Marcia.

As she said it, they heard Dad shouting from the bathroom. "What the devil has happened to the heating boiler? It's gone *out*!"

Chair Person's feet blundered in the passage. "Er, hn hm, I appeared to get very cold in the night," his voice brayed. "But I happen to know a lot about snuffle technology. I adjusted the boiler. High-speed gas for warmth and snuffle efficiency."

"It's not gas, it's *oil*!" Dad roared. "You turned the whole system off, you fool!"

"Oil?" said Chair Person, not in the least worried. "Liquid engineering. I happen to know—hn hm—that both oil and gas come from the North Sea, where giant oil rigs—"

Dad made a sort of gargling noise. His feet hammered away downstairs. There were a few clangs and a clank and the sound of Dad swearing. After a while the house started to get warm again. The frost on the window slid away to the corners and turned to water.

Marcia looked at Simon. She wanted to say that Simon was the one who had said Chair Person would be better today. But she could see Simon knew he was just the same. "Do you still think he'll learn?" she said.

"I *think* so," said Simon, though he knew he was going to have to work quite hard to go on feeling sorry for Chair Person at this rate.

4

Coffee Morning

Chair Person ate four boiled eggs and half a packet of shredded wheat for breakfast. He drank what was left of the milk with loud, slurping sounds while he told them about oil rigs and then about shipbuilding. "Er, hn hm," he said. "Studies at the dockyards reveal that less than ten snuffle slurp percent of ships now being built are launched by the Queen. Oh, dear, I appear to have drunk all your—hn hm—milk."

Dad jumped up. "I'll buy more milk," he said. "Give me a list of all the other things you want for the coffee morning and I'll buy them, too."

"Coward!" Mum said bitterly when Dad had gone off with orders to buy ten cake mixes, milk, and cookies. She was in a great fuss. She told Chair Person to go upstairs and watch television. Chair Person went crawlingly humble and went away saying he knew he was—hn hm—being a lot of trouble. "And I hope he stays there!" said Mum. She made Simon help in the kitchen and told Marcia to find twenty chairs—which were all the chairs in the house—and put them in a circle in the living room. "And I suppose it's too much to hope that Auntie Christa will come in and help!" Mum added.

It *was* too much to hope. Auntie Christa did turn up. She put her head around the back door as Simon was fetching the sixth tray of cakes out of the oven. "I won't interrupt," she said merrily. "I have to dash down to the Community Hall. Don't forget you're all helping with the party this evening." And away she went and did not come back until Mum and Simon had heaped cakes on ten plates and Dad and Marcia were counting coffee cups. "You *have* done well!" Auntie Christa said. "We must have African Aid here every week."

Dad started to groan and then stopped, with a thoughtful look on his face.

The doorbell began ringing. A lot of respectable elderly ladies arrived, and one or two respectable elderly men, and then the Vicar. They each took one of the twenty seats and chatted politely while Simon and Marcia went around with cakes and cookies and Mum handed out coffee. When everyone had a cup and a plate of something, the Vicar cleared his throat—a bit like Chair Person but nothing like so loudly.

"Er, hm," he said. "I think we should start."

The door opened just then, and Dad ushered in Chair Person.

"Oh, *no!*" said Mum, looking daggers at Dad.

Chair Person stood, pawing at the air, and looked around at the respectable people in a very satisfied way. He had found Dad's best shiny brown shoes to wear and Simon's football socks, which looked decidedly odd with his striped suit. The respectable people stared, at the shoes, the socks, the hairy legs above that, at the stain on his striped stomach, and then at the smashed-hedgehog beard. Even Auntie Christa stopped talking and looked a little dazed.

"Er, hn hm," brayed Chair Person twice as loudly as the Vicar. "I am—hn snuffle—Chair Person. How kind of you all to come and—hn hm—meet me. These good people"—he nodded and waved arms at Dad and Mum—"have been honored to put up with me, but they are only small stupid people who do not matter."

The slightly smug smile on Dad's face vanished at this.

"I shall—hn hm—talk to people who matter," said Chair Person. He lumbered across the room, bumping into everything he passed. Ladies hastily got coffee cups out of his way. He stopped in front of the Vicar and breathed heavily. "Could I trouble you to move?" he said.

"Eh?" said the Vicar. "Er—"

"Er, hn hm, you appear to be sitting in my seat," said Chair Person. "I am Chair Person. I am the one who shall talk to—hn hm—the government. I shall be running this meeting."

The Vicar got out of the chair as if it had scalded him and backed away. Chair Person sat himself down and looked solemnly around.

"Coffee," he said. "Er, hn hm, cakes. While the rest of the world starves."

Everyone shifted and looked uncomfortably at their cups.

In the silence Chair Person looked at Mum. "Hn hm," he said. "Maybe you have not noticed that you've not given me—hn hm—coffee or cakes."

"Is *that* what you meant?" said Mum. "I thought after all the breakfast you ate—"

"I meant—hn hm—that we are here to feast and prove that we at least have enough to eat," said Chair Person. While Mum was angrily pouring coffee into the cracked cup that was the last one in the cupboard, he turned to the nearest lady. "I decided to grow a beard," he said, "to show I am—hn hm—important to the ecology. It makes my face look snuffle grand."

The lady stared at him. Auntie Christa said loudly, "We are here to talk about Africa, Mr. Chair Person."

"Er, hn hm," said Chair Person. "I happen to know a lot about Africa. The government should act to make sure that the African—hn hm—elephant does not die out."

"We were not going to talk about elephants," the Vicar said faintly.

"The snuffle gorilla is an endangered animal, too," said Chair Person. "And the herds of—hn hm—wildebeest are not what they were in the days of Dr. Livingstone, I presume. Drought afflicts many animals—I appear to have drunk all my coffee—and famine is poised to strike." And he went on talking, mixing up about six different television programs as he talked. The Vicar soon gave up trying to interrupt, but Auntie Christa kept trying to talk, too. Every time she began, Chair Person went "ER, HN HM!" so loudly that he drowned her out, and took no notice of anything she said. Marcia could not help thinking that Chair Person must have stood in the living room picking up hints from Auntie Christa for years. Now he was better at not letting other people talk than Auntie Christa was.

In the meantime Chair Person kept eating cakes and asking for more coffee. The respectable people, in a dazed sort of way, tried to keep up with Chair Person, which meant that Simon and Marcia were kept very busy carrying cups and plates. In the kitchen Mum was baking and boiling the kettle nonstop, while Dad grimly undid packets and mixed cake mix after cake mix.

By this time Simon was finding it hard to be sorry for Chair Person at all. "I didn't know you thought you were so important," he said as he brought Chair Person another plate of steaming buns.

"This must be—hn hm—reported to Downing Street," Chair Person told the meeting, and he interrupted himself to say to Simon, "That is because I—er, hn hm—always take care to be polite to people like you who don't snuffle count . . . I shall make you feel good by praising these cakes. They are snuffle country soft and almost as mother used to make." And turning back to the dazed meeting, he said, "Ever since the days of the pharaohs—hn hm—Egypt has been a place of snuffle mystery and romance."

There seemed nothing that would ever stop him. Then the doorbell rang. Unfortunately Dad, Mum, Marcia, and Simon were all in the kitchen when it rang, pouring the last of the cake mix into paper cases. By the time Marcia and Dad got to the front door, Chair Person had got there first and opened it.

Two men were standing outside holding a new armchair. It was a nice armchair, a nice plain blue, with a pleasant look on the cushion at the back where Chair Person's face had come from. Marcia thought Mum and Dad had chosen well.

"I—er, hn hm—I said take that thing away," Chair Person told the men. "This house is not big enough for snuffle both of us. The post is—hn hm—filled. There has been a mistake."

"Are you sure? This is the right address," one of the men said.

Dad pushed Chair Person angrily aside. "Mind your own business!" he said. "No, there's no mistake. Bring that chair inside."

Chair Person folded his waving arms. "Er, hn hm. My rival enters this house over my dead body," he said. "This thing is bigger than snuffle both of us."

While they argued, Auntie Christa was leading the coffee morning people in a rush to escape through the kitchen and out of the back door. "I do think," the Vicar said kindly to Mum as he scampered past, "that your eccentric uncle would be far happier in a Home, you know."

Mum waited until the last person had hurried through the back door. Then she burst into tears. Simon did not know what to do. He stood staring at her. "A Home!" Mum wept. "I'm the one who'll be in a Home if someone doesn't *do* something!"

5

Junk Shop

Chair Person got his way over the new chair, more or less. The men carried it to the garden shed and shoved it inside. Then they left, looking almost as bewildered and angry as Dad.

Marcia, watching and listening, was quite sure now that Chair Person had been learning from Auntie Christa all these years. He knew just how to make people do what he wanted. But Auntie Christa did not live in the house. You could escape from her sometimes. Chair Person seemed to be here to stay.

"We'll have to get him turned back into a chair somehow," she said to Simon. "He's not getting better. He's getting worse and worse."

Simon found he agreed. He was not sorry for Chair

Person at all now. "Yes, but *how* do we turn him back?" he said.

"We could ask old Mr. Pennyfeather," Marcia suggested. "The conjuring set came from his shop."

So that afternoon they left Mum lying on her bed upstairs and Dad moodily picking up frostbitten apples from the grass. Chair Person was still eating lunch in the kitchen.

"Where does he put it all?" Marcia wondered as they hurried down the road.

"He's a chair. He's got lots of room for stuffing," Simon pointed out.

Then they both said, "Oh, *no!*"

Chair Person was blundering up the road after them, panting and snuffling and waving his arms. "Er, hn hm, wait for me!" he called out. "You appear to have snuffle left me behind."

He tramped beside them, looking pleased with himself. When they got to the shops where all the people were, shoppers turned to stare as Chair Person clumped past in Dad's shoes. Their eyes went from the shoes, to the football socks, and then to the short, striped suit, and then on up to stare wonderingly at the smashed-hedgehog beard. More heads turned every time Chair Person's voice brayed out, and of course, he talked a lot. There was something in every shop to set him going.

At the bread shop he said, "Er, hn hm, those are Sam Browne's lusty loaves. I happen to know snuffle they are nutrition for the nation."

Outside the supermarket he said, "Cheese to please, you can snuffle freeze it, squeeze it and—er, hn hm—there is Tackley's tea, which I happen to know has over a thousand holes to every bag. Flavor to snuffle savor."

Outside the wine shop his voice went up to a high roar. "I—hn hm—see Sampa's Superb sherry here, which is for ladies who like everything silken snuffle smooth. And I happen to know that in the black bottle there is—hn hm—a taste of Olde England. There is a stagecoach on the—hn hm—label to prove it. And look, there is Bogans—hn hm—beer, which is, of course, for Men Only."

By now it seemed to Simon and Marcia that everyone in the street was staring. "You don't want to believe everything the ads say," Simon said uncomfortably.

"Er, hn hm, I appear to be making you feel embarrassed," Chair Person brayed, louder than ever. "Just tell me snuffle if I am in your way and I will snuffle go home."

"Yes, do," they both said.

"I—er, hn hm—wouldn't dream of pushing in where I am snuffle not wanted," Chair Person said. "I would—hn hm—count it a favor if you tell me snuffle truthfully every time you've had enough of me. I—er, hn hm—know I must bore you quite often."

36

By the time he had finished saying this they had arrived at old Mr. Pennyfeather's junk shop. Chair Person stared at it.

"We—er, hn hm—don't need to go in there," he said. "Everything in it is old."

"You can stay outside then," said Marcia.

But Chair Person went into another long speech about not wanting to be—hn hm—a trouble to them and followed them into the shop. "I—er, hn hm—might get lost," he said, "and then what would you do?"

He bumped into a cupboard.

Its doors opened with a *clap*, and a stream of horse brasses poured out: clatter, *clatter*, CLATTER!

Chair Person lurched sideways from the horse brasses and walked into an umbrella stand made out of an elephant's foot,

which fell over—*crash* CLATTER—

against a coffee table with a big jug on it,

which tipped and slid the jug off—CRASH, splinter, splinter—

and then fell against a rickety bookcase,

which collapsed sideways, spilling books—thump, thump, thump-thump-thump—

and hit another table loaded with old magazines and music,

which all poured down around Chair Person.

It was like dominoes going down.

The bell at the shop door had not stopped ringing before Chair Person was surrounded in knocked-over furniture and knee-deep in old papers. He stood in the midst of them, waving his arms and looking injured.

By then Mr. Pennyfeather was on his way from the back of the shop, shouting, "Steady, steady, steady!"

"Er, hn hm—er, hn hm," said Chair Person, "I appear to have knocked one or two things over."

Mr. Pennyfeather stopped and looked at him, in a knowing, measuring kind of way. Then he looked at Simon and Marcia. "He yours?" he said. They nodded. Mr. Pennyfeather nodded, too. "Don't move," he said to Chair Person. "Stay just where you are."

Chair Person's arms waved as if he were conducting a very large orchestra, several massed choirs, and probably a brass band or so as well. "I—er, hn hm, er, hn hm—I—er, hn hm—" he began.

Mr. Pennyfeather shouted at him, "*Stand still! Don't move, or I'll have the springs out of you and straighten them for toasting forks!* It's the only language they understand," he said to Simon and Marcia. "STAND STILL! YOU HEARD ME!" he shouted at Chair Person.

Chair Person stopped waving his arms and stood like a statue, looking quite frightened.

"You two come this way with me," said Mr. Pennyfeather, and he took Simon and Marcia down to the far end of his shop, between an old ship's wheel and a carved maypole, where there was an old radio balanced on a tea chest. He turned the radio up loud so that Chair Person could not hear them. "Now," he said, "I see you two got problems to do with that old conjuring set. What happened?"

"It was Auntie Christa's fault," said Marcia.

"She let the crystal ball drip on the chair," said Simon.

"*And* tapped it with the magic wand," said Marcia.

Mr. Pennyfeather scratched his withered old cheek. "My fault, really," he said. "I should never have let her have those conjuring things, only I'd got sick of the way the stuff in my shop would keep getting lively. Tables dancing and such. Mind you, most of my furniture only got a drip or so. They used to calm down after a couple of hours. That one of yours looks as though he got a right dousing—or maybe the wand helped. What was he to begin with, if you don't mind my asking?"

"Our old armchair," said Simon.

"Really?" said Mr. Pennyfeather. "I'd have said he was a sofa, from the looks of him. Maybe what you had was an armchair with a sofa opinion of itself. That happens."

"Yes, but how can we turn him *back*?" said Marcia.

Mr. Pennyfeather scratched his withered cheek again. "This is *it*," he said. "Quite a problem. The answer must be in that conjuring set. It wouldn't make no sense to have that crystal ball full of stuff to make things lively without having the antidote close by. That top hat never got lively. You could try tapping him with the wand again. But you'd do well to sort through the box and see if you couldn't come up with whatever was put on the top hat to stop it getting lively at all."

"But we haven't got the box," said Simon. "Auntie Christa's got it."

"Then you'd better borrow it back off her quick," Mr. Pennyfeather said, peering along his shop to where Chair Person was still standing like a statue. "Armchairs with big opinions of theirselves aren't no good. That one could turn out a real menace."

"He already *is*," said Simon.

Marcia took a deep, grateful breath and said, "Thanks awfully, Mr. Pennyfeather. Do you want us to help tidy up your shop?"

"No, you run along," said Mr. Pennyfeather. "I want him out of here before he does any worse." And he shouted down the shop at Chair Person, "Right, you can move now! Out of my shop *at* the double, and wait in the street!"

Chair Person nodded and bowed in his most crawlingly humble way and waded through the papers and out of the shop. Simon and Marcia followed, wishing they could manage to shout at Chair Person the way Mr. Pennyfeather had. But maybe they had been brought up to be too polite. Or maybe it was Chair Person's sofa opinion of himself. Or maybe it was just that Chair Person was bigger than they were and had offered to eat them when he first came out of the shed. Whatever it was, all they seemed to be able to do was to let Chair Person clump along beside them, talking and talking, and try to think how to turn him into a chair again.

They were so busy thinking that they had turned into their own road before they heard one thing that Chair Person said. And that was only because he said something new.

"*What* did you say?" said Marcia.

"I said," said Chair Person, "I appear—er, hn hm, snuffle—to have set fire to your house."

Both their heads went up with a jerk. Sure enough, there was a fire engine standing in the road by their gate. Firemen were dashing about unrolling hoses. Thick black smoke was rolling up from behind the house, darkening the sunlight and turning their roof black.

Simon and Marcia forgot Chair Person and ran.

Mum and Dad, to their great relief, were standing in the road beside the fire engine, along with most of the neighbors. Mum saw them. She let go of Dad's arm and rushed up to Chair Person.

"All right. Let's have it," she said. "What did you do *this* time?"

Chair Person made bowing and hand-waving movements, but he did not seem sorry or worried. In fact, he was looking up at the surging clouds of black smoke rather smugly. "I—er, hn hm—was thirsty," he said. "I appear to have drunk all your orange juice and lemon squash and the stuff snuffle from the wine and whiskey bottles, so I—hn hm—put the kettle on the gas for a cup of tea. I appear to have forgotten it when I went out."

"You fool!" Mum screamed at him. "It was an electric kettle, anyway!" She was angry enough to behave just like Mr. Pennyfeather. She pointed a finger at Chair Person's striped stomach. "I've had enough of you!" she shouted. "You stand there and don't *dare* move! Don't *stir*, or I'll—I'll—I don't know what I'll do, but you won't like it!"

And it worked, just as it did when Mr. Pennyfeather shouted. Chair Person stood still as an overstuffed statue. "I—hn hm—appear to have annoyed you," he said in his most crawlingly humble way.

He stood stock-still in the road all the time the firemen were putting out the fire. Luckily only the kitchen was burning. Dad had seen the smoke while he was picking up apples in the garden. He had been in time to phone the fire brigade and get Mum from upstairs before the rest of the house caught fire. The firemen hosed the blaze out quite quickly. Half an hour later Chair Person was still standing in the road and the rest of them were looking around the ruined kitchen.

Mum gazed at the melted cooker, the crumpled fridge, and the charred stump of the kitchen table. Everything was black and wet. The vinyl floor had bubbled. "Someone get rid of Chair Person," Mum said, "before I murder him."

"Don't worry. We're going to," Simon said soothingly.

"But we have to go and help at Auntie Christa's children's party in order to do it," Marcia explained.

"I'm not going," Mum said. "There's enough to do here—and I'm not doing another thing for Auntie

Christa—not after this morning!"

"Even Auntie Christa can't expect us to help at her party after our house has been on fire," Dad said.

"Simon and I will go," Marcia said. "And we'll take Chair Person and get him off your hands."

6

Party Games

The smoke had made everything in the house black and gritty. Simon and Marcia could not find any clean clothes, but the next-door neighbors let them use their bathroom and kindly shut up their dog so that Marcia would not feel nervous. The neighbors on the other side invited them to supper when they came back. Everyone was very kind. More kind neighbors were standing anxiously around Chair Person when Simon and Marcia came to fetch him. Chair Person was still standing like a statue in the road.

"Is he ill?" the lady from Number 27 asked.

"No, he's not," Marcia said. "He's just eccentric. The Vicar says so."

Simon did his best to imitate Mr. Pennyfeather.

"Right," he barked at Chair Person. "You can move now. We're going to a party."

Though Simon sounded to himself just like a nervous person talking loudly, Chair Person at once started snuffling and waving his arms about. "Oh—hn hm—good," he said. "I believe I shall like a party. What snuffle party is it? Conservative, Labour, or that party whose name keeps changing? Should I be—hn hm—sick of the moon or over the parrot?"

At this, all the neighbors nodded to one another. "*Very* eccentric," the lady from Number 27 said as they all went away.

Simon and Marcia led Chair Person toward the Community Hall trying to explain that it was a party for Caring Society Children. "And we're supposed to be helping," Marcia said. "So do you think you could try to behave like a proper person for once?"

"You—hn hm—didn't have to say *that*!" Chair Person said. His feelings were hurt. He followed them into the hall in silence.

The hall was quite nicely decorated with bunches of balloons and full of children. Simon and Marcia knew most of the children from school. They were surprised they needed caring for, most of them seemed just ordinary children. But the thing they looked at mostly was the long table at the other end of the room. It had a white cloth on it. Much of it was covered with food: jellies, cakes, crisps, and big bottles of Coke. But at one end was the pile of prizes, with the green teddy on top. The conjuring set, being quite big, was at the bottom of the pile. Simon and Marcia were glad, because that would mean it would be the last prize anybody won. They would have time to look through the box.

Auntie Christa was in the midst of the children, trying to pin someone's torn dress. "There you are at last!" she called to Simon and Marcia. "Where are your mother and father?"

"They couldn't come—we're awfully sorry!" Marcia called back.

Auntie Christa rushed out from among the children. "Couldn't come? Why *not*?" she said.

"Our house has been on fire—" Simon began to explain.

But Auntie Christa, as usual, did not listen. "I think that's extremely thoughtless of them!" she said. "I was counting on them to run the games. Now I shall have to run them myself."

While they were talking, Chair Person lumbered into the crowd of children, waving his arms importantly. "Er, hn hm, welcome to the party," he brayed. "You are all honored to have me here because I am—snuffle—Chair Person and you are only children who need caring for."

The children stared at him resentfully. None of them thought of themselves as needing care. "Why is he wearing football socks?" someone asked.

Auntie Christa whirled around and stared at Chair Person. Her face went quite pale. "Why did you bring *him*?" she said.

"He—er—he needs looking after," Marcia said, rather guiltily.

"He just nearly burned our house down," Simon tried to explain again.

But Auntie Christa did not listen. "I shall speak to your mother very crossly indeed!" she said, and ran back among the children, clapping her hands. "Now listen, children. We are going to play a lovely game. Stand quiet while I explain the rules."

"Er, hn hm," said Chair Person. "There appears to be a feast laid out over there. Would it snuffle trouble you if I started eating it?"

At this, quite a number of the children called out, "Yes! Can we eat the food now?"

Auntie Christa stamped her foot. "No, you may *not*! Games come first. All of you stand in a line, and Marcia, bring those beanbags from over there."

Once Auntie Christa started giving orders, Chair Person became quite obedient. He did his best to join in the games. He was hopeless. If someone threw him a

beanbag, he dropped it. If he threw a beanbag at someone else, it hit the wall or threatened to land in a jelly.
The team he was in lost every time.

So Auntie Christa tried team Follow My Leader, and
that was even worse. Chair Person lost the team he was
with and galumphed around in small circles on his own.
Then he noticed that everyone was running in zigzags
and ran in zigzags, too. He zagged when everyone else
zigged, bumping into people and treading on toes.

"Can't you stop him? He's spoiling the *game*!" children
kept complaining.

Luckily Chair Person kept drifting off to the table to
steal buns or help himself to a pint or so of Coke. After
a while Auntie Christa stopped rounding him up back
into the games. It was easier without him.

But Simon and Marcia were getting worried. They
were being kept so busy helping with teams and fetching
things and watching in case people cheated that they had
no time at all to get near the conjuring set. They watched
the other prizes go. The green teddy went first, then the
broken train, and then other things, until half the pile
was gone.

Then at last Auntie Christa said the next game was
Musical Chairs. "Simon and Marcia will work the record
player, and I'll be the judge," she said. "All of you bring
one chair each into the middle. *And* you!" she said,

grabbing Chair Person away from where he was trying to eat a jelly. "This is a game even you can play."

"Good," Simon whispered as he and Marcia went over to the old, old record player. "We can look in the box while the music's going."

Marcia picked up an old scratched record and set it on the turntable. "I thought we were never going to get a chance!" she said. "We can give them a good long go with the music first time." She carefully lowered the lopsided stylus. The record began:

Here we go gathering click *in May,*
Click *in May, nuts in* click . . .

and all the children danced cautiously around the chairs, with Chair Person prancing in their midst, waving his arms like a lobster.

Simon and Marcia ran to the table and pulled the conjuring box out from under the other prizes. The crystal ball was still leaking. There was quite a damp patch on the tablecloth. But the wand was lying on top, when they opened the box, still wrapped in flags. Simon snatched it up. Marcia ran back and lifted the stylus off the record. There was a stampede for chairs.

Chair Person, of course, was the one without a chair. Simon had expected that. He followed Chair Person and gave him a smart tap with the wand as Chair Person blundered up the line of sitting children. But the wand did not seem to work. Chair Person pushed the smallest girl off the end chair and sat in it himself.

"I saw that! You were out!" Auntie Christa shouted, pointing at him.

Chair Person sat where he was. "I—er, hn hm—appear to be sitting in a chair," he said. "That was the snuffle rule as I understand it."

Auntie Christa glared. "Start the game again," she said.

Simon tapped Chair Person on the head with the wand before everyone got up, but that did not seem to work either. "What shall we *do*?" he whispered to Marcia, as they hurried back to the record player.

"Try it without the flags," Marcia whispered back. She lowered the stylus again.

"*Here we go gathering* click *in May*," the record began as Simon dashed over to the table, unwrapping the string of flags from the wand as he went. He was just putting the flags back in the box, when the table gave a sort of wriggle and stamped one of its legs.

Simon beckoned Marcia madly. The box must have been standing on the table for quite a long time. The stuff from the crystal ball had leaked down into the table and spread along the tablecloth to the food. The tablecloth was rippling itself, in a sly, lazy way. As Marcia arrived, one of the jellies spilled its way up to the edge of its cardboard bowl and peeped timidly out.

"It's *all* getting lively," Simon said.

"We'd better take the crystal ball to the toilet and drain it away," Marcia said.

"No!" said Simon. "Think what might happen if the toilet gets lively! Think of something else."

"Why should *I* always have to be the one to think?" Marcia snapped. "Get an idea for yourself for once!" She knew this was unfair, but by this time she was in as bad a fuss as Mum.

Here the record got as far as "*Who shall we* click *to* click *him away?*" and stuck. "*Who shall we* click, *who shall we* click . . ."

Marcia raced for the record and took it off. Simon raced among the stampede toward Chair Person and hit him with the unwrapped wand. Again nothing happened. Chair Person pushed a boy with a leg brace off the end chair and sat down. Auntie Christa said angrily, "This is *too* bad! Start the game again."

Marcia put the stylus down on the beginning of the record a third time. "I'd better stay and do this," she said. "You go and search the box—quickly, before we get landed with Table Person and Jelly Person as well!"

Simon sped to the table and started taking things out

of the conjuring box—first the flags, then the dripping hat with the crystal ball in it. After that came a toy rabbit, which was perhaps meant to be lively when it was fetched out of the hat. Yet, for some reason, it was just a toy. None of the things in the box was more than just wet. Simon took out a sopping leather wallet, three soaking packs of cards, and a dripping bundle of colored handkerchiefs. They were all just ordinary. That meant that there *had* to be a way of stopping things getting lively, but search as he would, Simon could not find it.

As he searched, the cracked music stopped and started and the table stamped one leg after another in time to it. Simon glanced at the game. Chair Person had found another way to cheat. He simply sat in his chair the whole time.

"I'm counting you out," Auntie Christa kept saying. And Chair Person went on sitting there with his smashed-hedgehog chin pointing obstinately to the ceiling.

Next time Simon looked, there were only two chairs left beside Chair Person's and three children. "We'll have tea after this game," Auntie Christa called as Marcia started the music again.

Help! thought Simon. The wobbling, climbing jelly was half out of its bowl, waving little feelers. Simon turned the whole box out onto the jigging table. All sorts of things fell out. But there was nothing he could see that looked useful—except perhaps a small wet pillbox. There was a typed label on its lid that said "DISAPPEARING BOX." Simon hurriedly opened it.

It was empty inside, so very empty that he could not see the bottom. Simon put it down on the table and stared into it, puzzled.

Just then the table got livelier than ever from all the liquid Simon had emptied out of the conjuring box. It started to dance properly. The tablecloth got quite lively, too, and stretched itself in a long, lazy ripple. The two things together rolled the hat with the crystal in it across the tiny, empty pillbox.

There was a soft WHOP. The hat and the crystal were sucked into the box. And they were gone. Just like that. Simon stared.

The table was still dancing and the tablecloth was still rippling. One by one, and very quickly, the other things from the conjuring box were rolled and jigged across the tiny pillbox. WHOP went the rabbit, WHOP the wand, WHOP-WHOP the string of flags, and then all the other things WHOP WHOP WHOP, and they were all gone, too. The big box that had held the things tipped over and made a bigger WHOP. And that was gone as well, before Simon could move. After that the other prizes started to vanish WHOP WHOP WHOP. This seemed to interest the tablecloth. It put out a long, exploring corner toward the pillbox.

At that Simon came to his senses. He pushed the corner aside and rammed the lid on the pillbox before the tablecloth had a chance to vanish, too.

As soon as the lid was on, the pillbox was not there anymore. There was not even a whisper of a WHOP as it went. It was just gone. And the tablecloth was just a tablecloth, lying half wrapped across the few prizes left. And the table stood still and was just a table. The jelly slid back into its bowl. Its feelers were gone, and it was just a jelly.

The music stopped, too. Auntie Christa called out, "Well done, Philippa! You've won again! Come and choose a prize, dear."

"It's not fair!" somebody complained. "Philippa's won *everything!*"

Marcia came racing over to Simon as he tried to straighten the tablecloth. "Look, look! You *did* it! Look!"

Simon turned around in a dazed way. There were still two chairs standing in the middle of the hall after the game. One of them was an old shabby striped armchair. Simon was sure that was not right. "Who put—?" he began. Then he noticed that the chair was striped in sky blue, orange, and purple. Its stuffing was leaking in a sort of fuzz from its sideways top cushion. It had stains on both arms and on the seat. Chair Person was a chair again. The only odd thing out was that the chair was wearing football socks and shiny shoes on its two front legs.

"I'm not sure if it was the wand or the pillbox," Simon said.

They pushed the armchair over against the wall while everyone was crowding around the food.

"I don't think I could bear to have it on our bonfire after this," Marcia said. "It wouldn't seem quite kind."

"If we take its shoes and socks off," Simon said, "we could leave it here. People will probably think it belongs to the hall."

"Yes, it would be quite useful here," Marcia agreed.

Later on, after the children had gone and Auntie Christa had locked up the hall, saying over her shoulder, "Tell your mother and father that I'm not on speaking terms with either of them!" Simon and Marcia walked slowly home.

Simon asked, "Do you think he knew we were going to put him on our bonfire? Was he having his revenge on us?"

"He may have been," said Marcia. "He never talked about the bonfire, did he? But what was to stop him just *asking* us not to when he was a Person?"

"No," said Simon. "He didn't have to set the house on fire. I suppose that shows the kind of Person he was."

The four Grannies

1

Erg Gets an Idea

Erg's dad and Emily's mum found they had to go away to a conference for four days, leaving Erg and Emily at home.

"I want a house to come back to," said Erg's dad, thinking of the time Erg had borrowed the front door to make an underground fort in the garden.

"We'd better ask one of the grannies to come and look after them," said Emily's mum, knowing that if Erg did not borrow a thing, Emily could be trusted to fall over it and break it. Emily was younger than Erg, but she was enormous. She needed bigger shoes than Erg's dad.

There were four grannies to choose from, because Erg's dad and Emily's mum had both been divorced before they married one another.

Granny One was strict. She wore her hair scraped back from her forbidding face, and her favorite saying was, "Life is always saying No." Since Life did not have a voice, Granny One spoke for it, and said No about once every five minutes.

Granny Two was a worrier. She could worry about anything. She was fond of ringing up in the middle of the night to ask if Emily was getting enough vitamins, or—in her special, hushed worrying voice—if Erg ought to be sent to a Special School.

Granny Three was very rich and very stingy. She was the one Emily hated most. Granny Three always arrived with a large box of chocolates. She would give Erg's dad a chocolate, and Emily's mum a chocolate, and eat six herself, and take the rest of the box away with her when she went. Erg agreed with Emily that this was mean, but he thought Granny Three was more fun than the others, because she had a new car and different colored hair every time she came.

Granny Four was a saint. She was gentle and quavery and wrinkled. If Erg and Emily quarreled in front of her, or even spoke loudly, Granny Four promptly came over faint and had to have a doctor.

Granny Four was the one Erg and Emily chose to look after them. If you could avoid making Granny Four feel faint, she usually let you do what you wanted. But, when Emily's mum rang Granny Four to ask her, Granny Four was faint already. She had been let down over a Save the Children Bazaar and was too ill to come.

So, despite the shrill groans of Erg and the huge moans of Emily, Emily's mum phoned Granny One. To Erg's relief, Granny One was going on holiday and could not come either. So that left Granny Two, because Granny Three had never been known to look after anyone but herself. But Erg's dad phoned Granny Three, all the same, hoping she might pay for someone to look after Erg and Emily. Granny Three said she thought it was an excellent idea for Emily and Erg to look after themselves.

Erg's dad phoned Granny Two. "What!" exclaimed Granny Two, hushed and worried. "Leave dear Erg and poor little Emily all alone, for all that time!"

"But we're only going to Scotland for four days," Erg's dad protested.

"I know, dear," said Granny Two. "But I'm thinking of *you*. Scotland is covered with oil these days and *so* dangerous!"

Erg and Emily were not looking forward to Granny Two. They waved their parents off gloomily, and sat about waiting for Granny Two to arrive. She was a long time coming. Emily fidgeted round the living room like an impatient horse, knocking things over right and left. Erg felt an idea coming on. He wandered away to the kitchen to see what he could find.

All the food was wrapped up and carefully labeled so that Granny Two could find it, but Erg found a cookie tin. It had holes in the lid from the time he had started a caterpillar farm. Inside were the works of a clock he had once borrowed. It seemed a good beginning for an invention. He collected other things: an eggbeater, the blades off the mixer, a sardine tin opener, and a skewer. He took them all back to the living room and began fitting them together. The invention was already looking quite promising when the phone rang. Emily bounced up to answer it, and, quite naturally, she trod on the invention as she went and squashed it flat. Erg roared with rage.

It was Granny Two on the phone. "I'm terribly sorry, dear. I'd got halfway when I thought I'd left my kitchen tap on. I'm just setting out again now."

"*Was* your tap on?" asked Emily.

"No, dear. But just suppose it had been."

Emily went back to the living room to find Erg still roaring with rage. "Look what you've done! You've ruined my invention!"

Emily looked at the invention. It looked like a squashed cookie tin with eggbeaters sticking out of it.

"It's only a squashed cookie tin," she said. "And you ought to put those eggbeaters back."

But Erg had just discovered that the hand beater fitted beautifully into a split in the side of the cookie tin.

"You're not supposed to have any of them," said Emily. But Erg took no notice. He wound the handle of the eggbeater. The battered metal of the tin went in and out as if it were breathing, and the pieces of clock inside made a most interesting noise. Emily got annoyed at the way Erg had forgotten her. "Put those things *back, you horrible little boy!*" she roared.

She was trampling toward Erg to take the invention apart when a shocked voice said, "Emily! *Children!*"

They looked around to find Granny Four in the doorway. She was pale and quavery and threatening to faint.

2

More Grannies Arrive

Erg and Emily tried to stop Granny Four fainting by smiling politely. "I thought you weren't coming," said Erg.

"I couldn't leave you two poor children all alone," Granny Four said in a failing voice.

Emily and Erg looked at one another. Neither of them had quite the courage to say Granny Two was already on her way.

"Here you are, dear," Granny Four said to Emily. Shakily she held out a small, elderly book. "This will put you in a better frame of mind. It's a beautiful little book about a wicked little girl called Emily. You'll find it charming, dear."

Emily took the book. It was not the kind of gift you

could say thank you for easily. "I'll take it upstairs to read," Emily said, and thundered away so as not to seem ungrateful.

Erg was hoping heartily that Granny Four had something better for him. But it was not much better. It was a shiny red stick, narrower at one end than the other.

"I think it's a chopstick," said Granny Four. "It was in the bazaar." She must have seen from Erg's expression that he was not loving the chopstick particularly. She went white and leaned against the side of the door. "You can pretend it's a magic wand, dear," she said reproachfully.

Erg knew she would faint. He took the chopstick hurriedly and jammed it in one of the holes in his invention. It must have caught in the works of the clock inside the squashed tin, because when he wound the handle of the eggbeater, the skewer, the sardine tin opener, and the mixer blades all began to turn around, grating and clanking as they turned. It was much more interesting now.

Granny Four smothered a slight yawn and began to look healthier. "We can take such delight in simple things!" she said.

But just then a voice shouted, "Coo-ee!" and Granny Two staggered in. She had brought four bags of potatoes, two dozen oranges, and a packet of health food. Granny Four took in the situation and turned faint again. Granny Two took in Granny Four and sprang to her side.

"You shouldn't have come, dear. You look ready to collapse! Come upstairs and lie down and I'll make you a nice cup of tea." And she led Granny Four away.

Erg was rather pleased. It looked as if the two grannies could keep one another busy while he got on with his invention. He went into the kitchen again. This time he collected the cutters from the mincer, the handle of the hot tap, the knobs off the cooker, and the clip that held the bag of the vacuum cleaner together. Most of these things threaded very nicely onto the things stuck into the holes on top of the cookie tin. When Erg wound the eggbeater this time, the tap top, the mincer cutters, and the cooker knobs all twiddled round and round, quite beautifully. The works of the clock clanked. The tin breathed in and out. And everything ground and grated just like a real machine.

Erg was trying to find a place for the clip from the vacuum cleaner when he looked up into the outraged face of Granny One.

Granny One! Erg looked up again unbelievingly. She was really there. She was putting down her neat suitcase in order to fold her arms grimly.

"You're on holiday!" he said.

"I canceled my holiday," Granny One said grimly. "To look after you. Take all those things back to the kitchen at once."

"But you're on holiday," Erg argued. "You can have a holiday from saying No, if you like."

"Life is always saying No," said Granny One. "Take those things back."

"If Life is always saying No," Erg argued reasonably, "it's saying No to me taking them back, too."

But Granny One tapped the floor with her knobby shoe, quite impervious to reason. "I'm waiting. Do as you're told."

"Oh, bother you!" said Erg.

That was a mistake. It brought a storm down on Erg's head. It started with "Don't you speak to me like that!" and ended with Erg sullenly carrying the invention out into the hall to take it to pieces in the kitchen.

The noise fetched Granny Two down the stairs. She stared at Granny One. "What are *you* doing here?" said Granny Two.

"My duty," said Granny One. "I've come to look after the children."

"So have I," said Granny Two. "I can manage perfectly."

"Of course you can't," said Granny One. "You fuss all the time, and you spoil the children."

"And you," said Granny Two, "are cruel to them."

Granny One had her mouth open to make a blistering reply when Granny Four tottered down the stairs, faintly wringing her hands. Granny One pointed at her unbelievingly. "Is *she* here, too?"

"Yes, dear, but she can't manage on her own," said Granny Two.

"Indeed, I can!" Granny Four quavered, clinging to the stair rail.

"It's just as well I came," Granny One said grimly. "I see I shall have to look after the lot of you."

"I do not need looking after!" Grannies Two and Four said in chorus.

By this time it was clear to Erg that three grannies kept one another even busier than two. Much relieved, he went into the kitchen. There he put the hot tap top back, and the knobs from the cooker, because he knew Granny One would notice those. Then he went out of the back door and into the living room by the French window and hid the invention safely behind the sofa. Then he went out into the hall again. The grannies were still insulting one another.

"I didn't know you all hated one another," he said.

To his surprise, this stopped the argument at once. All the grannies turned and assured Erg that they loved one another very much. Then they turned and assured one another. After which they all went into the kitchen for a cup of tea.

Erg went back to work on his invention behind the sofa. The clip off the vacuum cleaner fitted nicely on the end of the sardine tin opener. But the invention needed something else to make it perfect. Erg could not think what it needed. He could not think clearly, because the grannies were now going up and down stairs, calling out about potatoes and rattling at doors.

Finally Granny Two came into the living room. "Erg, dear— Oh, dear! He's vanished, too. I'm so worried."

"No, I haven't," Erg said, bobbing up from behind the sofa. "I'm playing at hiding," he explained, before Granny Two could ask. "What's the matter?"

"Emily's locked herself in the bathroom, dear. Be a dear and go and get her out."

3
Emily Gets Converted

Erg sighed and went upstairs. But it was not a wasted journey. The thought of the bathroom put into his head exactly what would make the invention perfect. It needed glass tubes, with blue water bubbling in them, going *plotterta-plotterta* the way inventions did in films. He banged at the bathroom door.

"Go away!" boomed Emily from inside. She sounded tearful. "I'm busy. I'm reading Granny Four's book."

"Why are you doing it in there?" Erg asked.

"Because they keep interrupting and asking where to put potatoes and oranges."

"They want you to come out."

"I'm not going to," Emily boomed. "Not till I've read it. It's beautiful. It's ever so sad." Erg could hear her sobbing as he went away downstairs.

He went to the kitchen, where the grannies were sitting among mounds of potatoes and oranges, and told them Emily was reading.

He thought he would never understand grannies. One by one, they tiptoed to the bathroom, rattled the handle, and whispered there was a cup of tea outside. "And don't hurt your eyes, dear," Granny Two whispered. "I'm pushing a cookie under the door for you."

It seemed to be keeping them busy. Erg sat behind the sofa and got on with thinking how to make blue water go *plotterta-plotterta*. But he had still not worked it out when Granny Four came and quavered to him that Emily had not touched her tea. Nor had he when Granny Two came to tell him that Emily was ruining her eyes. Nor had he when Granny One came and told him to go out and get some nice fresh air.

Erg was annoyed. He wished he had thought of locking himself in the bathroom, too. And he was even more annoyed when Emily at last came out. She came straight to the sofa and crashed heavily down on it with her chin resting on the back.

"What are you making, dear brother?" she said in a sweet, cooing voice.

Erg looked up at her suspiciously. There were tear streaks down Emily's face and an expression on it even more saintly than Granny Four's. "What's the matter with you?" he said.

Emily turned her eyes piously to the ceiling. "I have taken a vow to be good, dear brother," she said. "It was that beautiful, sad book Granny Four gave me. The girl in it was called Emily, too, and she was terribly punished for her wickedness."

"Go away," said Erg. He was not sure he could bear it if Emily was going to be a saint as well as Granny Four.

"Ah, dear brother," cooed Emily, "do not spurn me. I must stay and pray for you. You have wickedly taken all the kitchen things for that Thing you're making."

"It's not a Thing!" Erg said angrily. Up till now he had not truly considered what his invention was, but Emily so annoyed him that he said rudely, "It's a prayer machine. You wind the handle and it answers your prayer."

"Sinful boy!" Emily said, with her eyes on the ceiling

again. "Let us pray. I pray that my beloved brother Erchenwald Randolph Gervase turns into a good boy—"

That was the most dreadful insult. Erg lost his temper. Usually when people said his string of terrible names, he hit them, but Emily was so much bigger than he was that he had never yet dared hit her. Instead, in a frenzy, he wound at the eggbeater. The squashed tin breathed in and out. The works of the clock ground and crunched inside. The chopstick revolved. The skewer twiddled. The sardine opener and the mincer cutters wobbled and whirled. Erg wound furiously: *pray pray pray praypraypray*. "Take Emily away!" he shouted. "I don't want her!"

In the midst of the noise, he thought he heard Emily stop being a saint and start shouting at him like she usually did. But he did not stop winding. *Pray pray pray praypraypray*.

When at last his arm became too tired to go on, he left off winding and looked up to glare at Emily. She was not there. In her place, with its chin resting on the back of the sofa, was a large yellow teddy bear.

4

A Large Yellow Teddy Bear

Erg stared at the teddy. The bear stared back at him. There was a sorrowful expression in its glass eyes and reproach written all over its yellow furry muzzle.

"Go away," Erg said to it. "You're not Emily. You're just pretending."

But the bear remained, leaning on the back of the sofa, staring reproachfully.

Erg took an alarmed look at his invention. *Could* it be a prayer machine? Could the chopstick perhaps really be a magic wand? These things just did not happen. On the other hand, he had never seen the teddy before in his life, and its furry face did look remarkably like Emily's. It was big, too, about as much too large for a teddy as Emily was for a girl. Erg tried not to think of what the grannies would say. He got up and searched the living room. Then he searched the garden. Emily was nowhere in either. Erg went out into the hall to search the rest of the house.

He stopped short. The front door was wide open. Granny Three was coming in through it, lugging bright red suitcases. Granny Three, of all people! Erg stared. Granny Three's hair was pale baby pink this time, and the new car outside in the road was bright snake green.

"There's no need to stare," Granny Three said to him. "I've come to look after you. Have you seen Emily?"

"No," said Erg, trying hard not to look guilty.

"Why not?" said Granny Three. "I've brought her

such a sweet dress." She put the suitcases down and picked up a dress from the hall stand. Erg blinked. It was a very small dress. It did not look as if it would fit the teddy bear, let alone Emily.

Still, this was the first time Granny Three had ever been known to give anyone anything.

The kitchen door opened, and Grannies Four, Two, and One looked out to see what was happening.

Granny Three took Granny Four in and, behind her, the unwelcoming faces of Grannies Two and One. She patted her pink hair and drew herself up tall. "I had to come," she said. "My conscience wouldn't let me leave those two poor children alone."

Erg was interested to hear that Granny Three thought she had a conscience. He always thought he inherited his lack of conscience from Granny Three. He looked at the other grannies to see what they thought.

Grannies Two and One did indeed draw breath as if they intended to say something thoroughly crushing, but then they looked at Erg and did not say it. Grannies Three and Four looked at Erg, too. All four put on sweet smiles.

And Erg felt horrible. He discovered he must have a conscience, too. He could not think why else he should feel so guilty about that teddy bear. Granny Three said brightly, "Well, what can I do? I brought my apron." Erg crept away from them upstairs and searched the rest of the house. But Emily was not anywhere. And when Erg went downstairs again, the teddy still sat accusingly on the sofa. Erg was forced to believe that he had indeed turned Emily into a teddy bear.

He dared not tell the grannies. When they called him to lunch, he said, "Emily's locked in the bathroom again."

"But she'll miss her dinner," quavered Granny Four.

Granny Three, who had settled in as if she had always lived there, said, "Then there'll be more for us. No, dear," she added to Granny One, "you must always mash potatoes with cream. I brought some cream."

Granny Two could not take the matter so calmly. "We must get Emily out before she grows up peculiar!" she said, and she set off upstairs to the bathroom.

Erg raced up with her and was just in time to wedge the landing carpet under the door so that it would not open. He left Granny Two there rattling and calling and raced down to the living room. The teddy still sat there, vast and yellow, on the sofa. But Erg felt it would be just like Emily to turn into something else while he was not looking. Then he might not be able to find her to turn her back. He decided to take the teddy in to lunch with him. That was terrible. Granny Three actually smiled kindly. Granny Four took the teddy and sat it in a chair of its own. "Is it a teddy-weddy then?" she said, and pretended to feed the teddy with mashed potato. Granny One kept looking from Erg to the teddy to Granny Four and snorting sarcastically. And when Granny Two came downstairs, she said, "Oh, the fairies have brought you a teddy! How exciting!"

In between all this, all the grannies wondered where Emily was and said she was growing up peculiar.

But halfway through lunch Erg noticed the glass salt cellar, and he saw the way out of his troubles. Let him put that salt cellar upside down, with a drinking straw in it. Let both be filled with blue water going *plotterta-plotterta*. And Erg knew the machine would answer his prayer and turn the teddy back into Emily again. The trouble was, could he do it before the grannies noticed that the teddy's reproachful face was exactly like Emily's?

Erg knew that he was going to have to keep all four grannies very busy.

5

How to Keep four Grannies Busy

When lunch was over, the grannies all put on aprons to wash up. Erg said he would take some lunch to Emily. Granny One sternly handed him two oranges.

"Eat those for vitamins," she said.

"That's right, dear," agreed Granny Two. "Push Emily's under the door for her."

Erg went upstairs and parked the teddy and the lunch in the bath. Then he wedged the door again and went down to the living room. He peeled both oranges and broke the peel into very small bits, which he scattered all over the carpet. But it takes a lot to keep four grannies busy. Erg was still gulping and feeling much too full of orange when Granny One escaped from the washing up and stood in the doorway, staring grimly at the bits of orange peel.

"I'll use the vacuum cleaner on it, shall I?" Erg said brightly.

"No, you will not," said Granny One. She went and got the vacuum cleaner herself and firmly plugged it in.

Erg watched expectantly as she switched it on. Since the clip that held the bag together was now part of the prayer machine, there was nothing to hold the dust in the cleaner at all. Dust came out in a cloud, like an explosion. Big wads of dirt followed it. And after that came orange peel, whirling and whizzing. Granny One switched the cleaner off in a hurry and screamed for help.

Granny Four hurried in and turned faint in the dust. Granny Three came and turned the vacuum cleaner upside down. All the rest of the dust fell out of it.

"I don't understand these things," Granny Three said fretfully. "Telephone for a man."

"Pull out the plug first!" gasped Granny Two, hastening to the scene. "There's electricity leaking into it all the time!"

"Nonsense!" snapped Granny One, coming to her senses. "Erg, what have you done to this machine?"

But Erg was already tiptoeing into the kitchen. Hastily he unscrewed the salt cellar and poured the salt into the nearest thing—which happened to be the sugar bowl. He snatched up a packet of transparent drinking straws. Finally, he turned the tap on over the half-finished washing up. It was not long before bubbly water was pouring over onto the floor. Erg turned the tap off again.

"Hey!" he yelled. "You left the tap running!"

This fetched all four grannies back at a gallop.

Satisfied, Erg went back into the dust-hung living room and collected the invention from behind the sofa. He took it up to the bathroom and locked himself in with it and the salt cellar and the straws and the teddy and Emily's lunch. He thought he had given himself an hour's peace at least.

But it takes more than dust and water to keep four grannies busy. Ten minutes later Granny Four was rattling at the bathroom door. "Emily, dear, are you all right?"

"It's me in here now," Erg called. "Emily's gone for a walk."

"Then could you let me in, dear?" Granny Four called back. "I'd like a little wash before I go for my rest."

"You can't *rest*!" Erg called. He was horrified. Next thing he knew, they would all be up here, fussing about with cups of tea and hot-water bottles and things.

"Why not, dear?" quavered Granny Four.

Erg cast about for a reason. His eye fell on the washing basket. "There's all the washing to do," he shouted. "I'll bring it downstairs for you, shall I?"

"I'd better go and tell them," quavered Granny Four, and tottered away.

But when Erg looked in the washing basket, it was empty. Nothing daunted, Erg took off the clothes he was wearing and put them in the basket. Grannies always said clothes were dirty when you had hardly worn them anyway. Then he went to Emily's room and his own and collected all the clothes he could find there. Erg unfolded them and scrunched them up in his hands and rammed them into the basket. Then he put on clean clothes and staggered downstairs with the basket.

"Here you are," he said, emptying the crumpled heap on the kitchen floor.

The four grannies were gathered there eating chocolates out of the box Granny Three had brought. They gave the heap various looks of suffering and dismay. Granny Four turned pale. Granny Two sprang up, saying she would fill the sink with nice hot water.

"You're allowed to use the washing machine," Erg said.

"Oh, no, dear," said Granny Two. "Electricity doesn't mix with water. It gets into the clothes, you know."

On reflection Erg thought that washing in the sink would keep them busier. He took the basket back to the bathroom. Then he undid the toilet cistern and took out the blue block in it to make the blue water that was to go *plotterta-plotterta*. Then he thought he had better check to see how busy the grannies were.

He peeped around the kitchen door to find them quite out of control again. Granny Three was standing in the heap of clothes sorting them out. She took up a shirt, shook it fiercely, and passed it to Granny One. "This is clean, too," she said. "I think someone has been making work for us."

"Quite right," said Granny One, holding the shirt up to the light. "Clean *and* ironed." She passed the shirt to Granny Two, who smoothed it out and folded it carefully and passed it to Granny Four. Granny Four turned to put the shirt on a large heap of others and saw Erg watching.

"Will you take these back upstairs, dear?" she said.

"All right," said Erg. "And then I'll bring down the rest of the washing, shall I?"

"*Is* there more?" Granny Three asked, transferring her angry look from the next shirt to Erg.

"Oh, yes," said Erg. There was going to be, if it killed him.

He went upstairs with the pile of clothes and locked himself in the bathroom again. At least, Erg thought, he had kept the grannies too busy to think of Emily for some time. But at the rate they were going, they would be asking about her any minute now.

Erg took the plate of lunch out of the bath and used it to dirty ten of the shirts in the pile. But though he spread the lunch very thinly and carefully with his toothbrush, it would not go around more than ten shirts. He found himself looking longingly at his invention where it sat in the washbasin. Even without the blue water, it had already worked quite well. Erg decided to give it another try.

He wound the eggbeater—*pray pray pray praypraypray*. The tin crunched in and out. The mixer blades, the skewer, and the sardine opener grated and revolved. The vacuum cleaner clip, the mincer cutters, and the chopstick wobbled and twirled. "Make the washing keep them busy," Erg said, winding away.

6

Erg's Invention Works

Erg's clean clothes had become quite well covered with lunch and the blue from the toilet block. He took them off and put them in the basket with the ten shirts. In their place, he put on the first clothes left in the heap: Emily's nightdress, his own jeans, and Emily's school shirt. Dressed in this flowing raiment, he went down to the living room to roll in the dust there. But Granny Four was there, feebly flicking with a duster.

"What are you doing, dear?"

"Playing oil sheiks," said Erg. He went out into the garden and rolled in a flower bed.

Granny Four was not in the living room when he came back. To Erg's horror, she met him outside the bathroom, carrying the teddy. "You forgot teddy-weddy, dear."

It was awful how the grannies kept getting out of control. Erg locked the door and took off the raiment. He put on the next things: Emily's tartan skirt and a frilly blouse. This time he took the teddy with him and wedged the bathroom door shut.

"What are you doing now, dear?" asked Granny Four.

"Playing North Sea oil," Erg explained. "The teddy is my sporran." He went and rolled in the flower bed again.

This time he got safely back to the bathroom. But he did not dare leave the teddy behind when he set out again in the next set of clothes, which were his own striped pajamas.

"I'm playing going to bed," he told Granny Four before she could ask, and went and rolled in the flower bed once more.

While he was rolling, Granny Two and Granny Three came into the garden with a basket of washing to hang on the clothesline. They were struggling to hold a ballooning skirt and a kicking pair of jeans in what seemed a very strong wind. Erg lay in the earth and watched. The skirt made a strong dive and almost got away. Both grannies caught it. It took them some time to get it pegged, and the dress they took up next seemed to be blowing even harder. Erg licked one finger and thoughtfully held it up. There was almost no wind. Yet the row of things on the line was flapping and struggling and kicking as if there were half a gale.

Interesting. But where was Granny One? Erg got up and went through the back door into the kitchen to check on Granny One. She was not there. But while Erg was looking around to make sure, the pile of wet washing on the draining board rolled heavily over and went *flap*, down onto the kitchen floor. Erg could see it oozing and trickling and spreading over the floor. He watched with interest. The washing was definitely working its way over toward the nearest heap of potatoes to get itself nice and dirty again.

Erg was delighted. The prayer machine worked! He went upstairs in his earthy pajamas, convinced that the chopstick really must be some kind of magic wand. He only needed to get the blue water working, and he could turn Emily back again.

But Granny One was outside the bathroom door, knocking and rattling at it. She turned and looked at Erg. He had rarely seen her look so grim.

"Take those pajamas off at *once*! What are you and Emily—?"

"The washing," Erg said hastily, "has fallen on the kitchen floor."

To his relief, Granny One pushed past him and went rushing downstairs to rescue the washing. Erg locked himself in the bathroom again and put the teddy back in the bath. He was beginning to feel that four grannies were too much for any boy to control. There was another annoying thing, too. There were no more of his own clothes left to wear. He had got them all dirty. He stayed in his pajamas and got down to work on the salt cellar at last.

He had the salt cellar nicely filled with blue water when he was interrupted again, by quivering shouts from the garden. Erg could not resist opening the bathroom window to look. There was washing all over the garden. Some of it was blowing and kicking in the gooseberry bushes. The rest of it was whirling around and around the lawn with all four grannies chasing it. Satisfied, Erg shut the window. He was determined to finish his invention.

It was much trickier than he had thought. The hole in the lid of the salt cellar was not big enough to get a straw through. Erg had to enlarge it with the skewer. And when he had got the straw to go through, he could not get the salt cellar to stand properly upside down on top of the machine. He had to bend open the blades of the electric mixer to hold it. And when he had done that, he still could not get the blue water to go *plotterta-plotterta*. It simply ran down through the straw and into the inside of the biscuit tin. When Erg wound the handle of the egg-beater, the water came out of the holes in the tin in blue showers.

"Bother!" said Erg.

As he put more blue water into the salt cellar, he began to feel that everything was getting out of hand. The machine would not work. The earthy front of his pajamas was blue and soaking, and so was most of the bathroom. And to crown it all, there was a new outcry from the grannies, from the kitchen this time. This was followed by feet on the stairs.

Next moment all four grannies were outside the bathroom door.

"Come out of there at once!" snapped Granny One.

"We're so worried, dear," hushed Granny Two.

"It was very unkind of you, dear," quavered Granny Four, "to fill the sugar bowl with salt."

But it was Granny Three who really alarmed Erg. "You know," she said, "that child has done something with Emily. I've not set eyes on her all the time I've been here."

Erg's eyes went guiltily to the sad face of the teddy in the bath.

Outside the door, Granny Two said, "I shall phone the fire brigade to get him out."

"And spank him when he is," Granny One agreed.

Erg listened to no more. He rammed the salt cellar and the straw back in place and wound the eggbeater. *Pray pray pray praypraypray.* Blue water squirted. The works of the clock sploshed. Around and around went the chopstick, the mixer blades, the salt cellar, the skewer, the sardine opener, the mincer cutters, the straw, and the clip off the vacuum cleaner.

"Only one granny," prayed Erg, winding desperately. "I can't manage more than one—please!"

7

Supergranny

There was a sudden silence outside the bathroom door. It's worked! Erg thought.

"Erg," said a large, quavery voice outside. "Erg, open this door."

"In a minute," Erg called.

The words were hardly out of his mouth when the bathroom door leaped and crashed open against the wall. The one granny Erg had asked for came in. Only one. But Erg stared at her in horror. She was six feet tall and huge all over. Her hair was the baby pink of Granny Three's. Her face was the stern face of Granny One, except that it wore the worried look of Granny Two. Her voice was the quavery voice of Granny Four, but it was four times as loud. Erg knew at a glance that what he had here was all four grannies in one. They had blended into Supergranny. He jumped up to run.

Supergranny swept toward Erg. With one hand she caught Erg's arm in a grip of steel. At the same time she was keenly scanning the rest of the bathroom.

"What is this mess?" she quavered menacingly. "And where is Emily?"

Erg dared not tell the truth. He avoided the teddy's accusing stare. "Emily went to play in the park," he said.

"Very well," said Supergranny. "We shall go and get her. Come along, dear."

"I can't go like this!" Erg protested, looking down at his earthy, blue, wet pajamas.

All the grannies were a little deaf when it suited them. Supergranny was superdeaf. "Come along, dear," she said. She plucked the teddy out of the bath and planted it in Erg's arms. "Don't forget teddy-weddy the fairies brought you." And she pulled Erg toward the door.

All Erg could think of was to spare one hand from the teddy and snatch up his invention from the washbasin as he was pulled away. Blue water from it trickled down his legs as Supergranny towed him downstairs, but Erg hung on to it grimly. As soon as he got a chance, he was going to wind the eggbeater again and get Supergranny sent to Mars—which was surely where she belonged.

But in the hall Supergranny's piercing eye fell on the

prayer machine. "You can't take that nasty thing, dear," she said. She dragged it away from Erg and dropped it on the floor. Miserably Erg tried dropping the teddy, too. But Supergranny picked it up again and once more planted it in Erg's arms. "Come along, dear."

Erg found himself in the street outside the house, in wet blue pajamas, with one hand clutching a huge teddy and the other in the iron grip of Supergranny. Behind him the front door crashed shut. Erg could tell by the noise that it had locked itself. "Have you got a key?" he said hopelessly.

All the grannies were a little vague at times, when it suited them. Supergranny was supervague. "I don't know, dear. Come along."

Erg knew he was locked out of the house and the prayer machine locked in. As a last hope, he tried lingering beside Granny Three's snake green car. "Can we drive to the park?"

But three of the grannies did not know how to drive, and that canceled out the one who did. "I don't know how to drive, dear," said Supergranny.

So Erg was forced to trot along the pavement beside Supergranny. They kept passing people Erg knew. Not one of these people spared a glance for Supergranny. It was as if they saw pink-haired superwomen every day. But every single person stared at Erg, and Erg's pajamas, and the huge teddy bear. Erg tried to keep an expression on his face of a boy playing woad-stained Ancient British convicts who had just slain a fierce teddy bear. But either that was too hard an idea for one face to express, or Erg did not express it very well. Almost everybody laughed.

Erg was glad when they reached the park and found it nearly empty, except for some girls on the swings.

Here Supergranny seemed to forget they had come to look for Emily. But that did not help Erg. Supergranny led him over to the slide and the swings. "You play, dear. Slide down the slide, while I rest my poor feet." She sat heavily on the nearest park bench.

Erg tried to defy her. "What if I don't slide down the slide?" he asked.

"Awful things happen to little boys who disobey," Supergranny quavered placidly.

Erg looked her in the steely eye and believed it. He leaned the teddy against the steps of the slide and began bitterly to climb up. He knew that when he got to the top, the girls on the swings would see him and laugh, too.

But when he got to the top of the slide, everyone had left the swings except one big girl. She was such a big girl that she had to swing with her legs stuck straight out in front of her. Erg sat at the top of the slide and stared.

That big girl was Emily!

Unbelievingly, Erg craned to look over his shoulder.

The big yellow teddy bear was still leaning against the steps of the slide. Had the invention perhaps not been a prayer machine after all? Erg looked hopefully over at the park bench. Supergranny still sat there. Her pink head was nodding in a superdoze.

Erg flung himself on the slide and shot down it. He shot off the bottom and raced across to the swings.

"Emily!" he panted. "What happened? Where did you go?"

Emily gave Erg an unfriendly look. "To have lunch with my friend Josephine," she said. "Dear brother," she added, and stood up against the swing ready to shoot forward on it and kick Erg in the stomach.

"Oh, be nice, please!" Erg begged her. "*Why* did you go?"

"Because you were so horrid to me," said Emily. "And then when I opened the front door, Granny Three was outside heaving a teddy out of her car, and I couldn't face her. I hate Granny Three. So I hid behind the door while she went to give you the teddy, and then I ran around to Josephine's."

So the teddy had come from Granny Three. It was all a terrible mistake. It was a natural mistake, perhaps, because Granny Three had never been known to give anyone anything before, but a mistake all the same. And to make matters worse, Supergranny had noticed Erg was not sliding. She sprang up and came scouring across to the swings, calling for Erg in a long, quavering hoot, like a magnified owl. It was such a noise, that people were running from the other end of the park to see what was the matter.

Erg watched her coming, feeling like a drowning man whose life is passing before him in a flash. The prayer machine had been working all along, he knew now. He had not asked it to turn Emily into a teddy bear, but he *had* asked it to send her away, and it did. It had not needed blue water. It had made the washing keep the grannies busy without. It did not even need to be a machine. It was the chopstick that did things. And, like all such things, Erg saw wretchedly, as Supergranny pounded toward him, it gave you three wishes, and he had used all three. He had no way of getting rid of Supergranny at all.

Emily stared at the vast, running Supergranny. "Whoever is that?"

"Supergranny," said Erg. "She's all of them, and she's after me. Please help me. I'll never be horrible to you again."

"Don't make promises you can't keep," said Emily, but she let go of the swing and stood up.

Supergranny pounded up. "*There* you are, Emily!" she hooted. "I've been *so* worried!"

"I was only in the park," Emily said. "I think we'll go home now." She was, Erg was interested to see, nearly as large as Supergranny.

"Yes, dear," Supergranny said, almost meekly. And when Emily picked up the teddy and gave it to her, Supergranny took it without complaining.

They set off home. "How are we going to get in?" Erg whispered to Emily. "She's locked us out."

"No problem. I took the key," Emily said.

Halfway home, Supergranny's feet began superkilling her. She came over superfaint and had to lean on Erg and Emily. Erg had to stand staggering under her huge weight on his own while Emily fetched out her key and opened the front door.

"Good Lord!" said Emily.

The hall was full of dirty clothes. Dry dirty clothes were now galloping and billowing downstairs. Wet dirty clothes were crawling soggily through from the kitchen. Emily shot a horrified look at Supergranny and went charging indoors to catch the nearest pair of dirty jeans. She tripped over the invention in the middle of the floor. She fell flat on her face. *Crunch. Crack.* The eggbeater rolled out from one side in two pieces. The chopstick rolled the other way, *snapped in half.*

"*Ow!*" said Emily.

The clothes flopped down and lay where they fell.

Supergranny's mighty arm seemed to disentangle itself between Erg's hands. It was suddenly four arms. Erg let go, and found himself surrounded by the four grannies, all staring into the hall, too.

"Get up, Emily!" snapped Granny One.

"Oh, Erg!" said Granny Two. "Out of doors in pajamas! You *are* growing up peculiar!"

"I shall take your teddy away again," said Granny Three. "Look at this mess! You don't deserve nice toys!"

"Let's have a nice cup of tea," quavered Granny Four. A thought struck her. She turned pale. "We can do without sugar," she said faintly. "It's better for us."

Erg looked from one to the other. He was very relieved and very grateful to Emily. But he knew he was not going to enjoy the next three days.

Who Got Rid of Angus Flint?

1

Angus flint Arrives

The day my sister, Cora, went away for a fortnight, a friend of Dad's called Angus Flint rang up out of the blue. He said his wife had just left him, so could he come and see us to cheer himself up? I don't know how my father came to have a friend like Angus Flint. They met at college. One of them must have been different.

Trust my awful little brother to ruin this paper, when Angus Flint stole all the rest. Pip's never recovered from Cora once rashly telling him he was a genius, and he thinks *he* was the one who got rid of Angus Flint. And I'm not awful. Things just happened to me.

Anyway, Dad was pleased Angus Flint had not forgotten him, so he said, "Yes," and then told Mum. Mum said, "Oh," in the blank sort of way I do when I find my brothers have pinched all my chocolate. Then she said, "I suppose he can have Cora's room." Imagine the way an Ancient Roman might say, "I suppose the lions can have my best friend," and you'll know how she said it.

That ought to have been a warning because Mum can like people no sane person can stand, but I was doing my piano practice, so I didn't attend. Miss Hawksmoore had given me an all-time big hit to work on called "Elfin Dance," and I was grinding my teeth at it. It sounds like two very glum medium-sized elephants trying to waltz. And the next number in my book is a top pop called "Fairy Rondeau." I only carry on because I like our piano so much. It's a great black grand piano that Mum bought for £10, cheap at £1,000 to our minds.

Pip can't decide what he's a genius *at*, but a little while ago he thought he might be a genius at playing the piano. He was doing his practice when Angus Flint arrived. But before that Pip and Tony—Tony's the brother between me and Pip—had been so glad that Cora was not around to henpeck them that they had celebrated by eating— Well, they wouldn't say what they had eaten, but Tony had come out in spots and been sick. Tony has the art of looking bland and vague when any misdeed happens. Mum thought he really was ill. When Angus Flint breezed in, Tony was in a chair in the sitting room with a bowl on his knees, and Mum was fussing.

Now this shows you what Angus Flint was like. Mum went to shake hands, saying she was sorry we were at sixes and sevens. And she explained that Tony had been taken ill.

Angus Flint said, "Then open the window. *I* don't want to get it." Those were his first words. He was square and stumpy, and he had a blank sort of face with a pout to it. His voice was loud and jolly.

Mum looked rather taken aback, but she slid the big window open a little and told Tony to go to bed. Dad asked Angus Flint to sit down. Angus Flint looked critically at the chairs and then sat in the best one. Dad had just begun to ask him where he was living these days when he bounced up again.

"This is a horribly uncomfortable chair. It's not fit to sit in," he said.

We hadn't done anything to it—though I wish we had now—it was just that the chair is one of Mum's bargains. All our furniture is bargains. But Pip looked at me meaningly and grinned, because I was shuddering. I can't bear anyone to insult a piece of furniture to its face. No matter how ugly or uncomfortable a chair or a table is, I don't think it should be told. It can't help it, poor thing. I know most of our furniture is hideous, and most of the chairs hurt you sooner or later, but there's no need to say so. But I don't think furniture can read, so I don't mind writing it.

Meanwhile, Dad got out of the chair Tony had been sitting in and suggested Angus Flint sit there. "Not that one," Angus Flint said. "That's infested with germs." He ignored all the other chairs and marched over to mine. "I want to sit down," he told me.

"Let Angus have your chair, Candida," Mum said.

I was furious, but I got up. People seem to think children have no rights. Pip made his Dying Chinaman face at me out of sympathy. Then he spun around on the piano stool, put his foot down on the loud pedal, and slammed into "How Shall I Thy True Love Know?" He's only got as far as that one. Tony says he'd know Pip's True Love anywhere: She's tone-deaf, with a stutter. She sounds worse with the loud pedal down.

Angus Flint was explaining in his loud, jolly voice that he'd taken up yoga since his wife left him. "You should all do yoga," he said. "It's very profound. It—" He stopped. Pip's True Love did a booming stutter and made a wrong note. Angus Flint roared, "Stop fooling with that piano, can't you? I'm talking."

"I've got to practice," Pip said.

"Not while I'm here," said Angus Flint. Then, before I could do anything, he sprang up and lifted Pip off the piano stool by his hair. It hurt Pip a lot—as I found out later for myself—but Pip managed to walk out of the room and not even look as if he were crying. My parents were stunned. They are just far too polite to guests. But I'm not.

"Do that again," I said, "and I shall personally see that you suffer."

All I got from Angus Flint was a blank, angry stare, and he went back to my chair. "This is a stupid chair," he said. "It's far too low." The Stare turned out to be his great weapon. He used it on anything he disliked. I kept getting it. Mostly it was over shutting the window. It's such a big window that when it's open, it's like having half the sitting room wall missing. I got colder and colder. I thought Tony's imaginary germs must have gone by now, so I got up and shut it.

Angus Flint did not stop his loud, jolly talk to Dad. He just got up and opened it again, talking all the time. I wasn't having that, so I got up and shut it. Angus Flint got up and opened it. I forget how many times we did this. In between, Angus Flint patted Menace. At least—I think he thought he was patting Menace, but Menace had every excuse to think he was being beaten.

"Good little dog, this," Angus Flint kept saying. Clout, thump!

"Don't hit him so hard," I said. I got the Stare again, so I got up and shut the window. While Angus Flint was opening it, Menace saved his ribs from being broken by squeezing under one of the cupboards and staying there. The space was small even for a dachshund.

2

The Smell in the Night

Menace didn't even come out from under the cupboard for supper, although it smelled delicious. Mum puts forth her best for visitors. Serve Tony right. He didn't want any.

Okay, okay. Mum's turn to be insulted. Angus Flint cut off a very small corner of his veal and nibbled at it like a rabbit. "This is nice, Margaret!" he said. He sounded thoroughly surprised, as if Mum were famous for cooking fried toads in snail sauce. Then he went on telling Dad that the Common Market was very profound. Mum was looking stormy and Dad seemed crushed by then. So I told Angus Flint that it wasn't profound at all. I didn't see why I shouldn't. After all, I am going to have the vote one day. But I got the Stare Treatment again, and then Angus Flint said, "I don't want to listen to childish nonsense."

I felt almost crushed, too. I was glad it was "Pass the Buck, Dad" on the telly. Pip and I did the washing up in order to see it, and Tony got out of bed—he'd watch that program if he was dying. We were all crouched around the television, ready to go, when Angus Flint came bustling in from the sitting room, where Mum was giving him polite coffee, and turned it over to the other channel. We all yelled at him.

"But you must watch 'Battered Brides'," he said. "It's very profound."

Profound, my left fibula! It's one of those awful series about girls sharing a flat. They undress a lot, which accounts for Angus Flint finding it profound. And he stood over the knob, too, so we couldn't turn it back without wrecking the telly. Tony was so furious that he stormed off to fetch Dad, and Pip and I raced after him.

Dad said, "I've had about enough of Angus!" which is strong language from him, and Mum said, "So have I!" and we all thundered back to the dining room.

And would you believe this? Angus Flint was standing on his head, doing yoga, watching "Battered Brides" upside down! You can't argue with someone who's upside down. We tried, but it just can't be done. Instead of a face, you have to talk to a pair of maroon socks—with a hole in one toe—nodding gently at eye level. The face you ought to be arguing with is on the floor, squashed and purple-looking and the wrong way up. And when you've talked to the socks for a while, the squashed face on the floor says, "I have to stay like this for ten more minutes," and you give up and go away. You have to.

We went to bed. I don't know how my parents managed for the rest of the evening, but I can guess. I heard them coming to bed. Dad was most earnestly probing to find out when Angus Flint intended to go. From the strong silence that followed, I gathered that Dad was getting the Stare Treatment, too.

In the middle of the night we were all woken up by a dreadful smell of burning. We thought the house was on fire at first. We were quite pleased, because that's one thing that's never happened to us yet. But the smell turned out to come from the kitchen. It was thick and black, like when you burn toffee.

So we all rushed to the kitchen. Angus Flint was there, calmly stuffing what looked like clean white sheets into the boiler.

"I had to burn these," he said. "They were covered with sugar or something."

"I could have washed them," said Mum.

She got the Stare. "They were ruined," said Angus Flint.

I looked at Pip. He was horribly disappointed. He had

always had such faith in sugar for beds. It's supposed to melt and make the victim sticky as well as scratchy. I've told him over and over again that it's worth taking the time to catch fleas off Menace. But I suppose Angus Flint would have burned the sheets for fleas, too.

He went to bed with clean sheets—Mum made his bed, because he never then, or any other time, did a thing himself—saying he would sleep late next morning. In fact, he got up before I did and ate my breakfast. Dad fled then. He said he had an urgent experiment at the lab. The coward. He saw me coming. And I couldn't complain to Mum either, because Angus Flint took her over and told her all morning how his wife had left him.

We heard quite a lot of it. The story had a sort of chorus which went, "Well, I couldn't stand for that, and I had to hit her." The chorus came so many times that the poor woman must have been black and blue. No wonder she left him! If I were her, I would have— Well, perhaps not, because, as we were swiftly finding out, Angus Flint was quite immune to anything ordinary people could do.

Mum was tired out by lunchtime. "Get lunch, Candida," she said. "I'm going out. I've got the—er—a meeting. I shan't be in till nearly seven."

That was how our heartless and cowardly parents left Tony, Pip, and me alone all and every day with Angus Flint.

3

Roller Skates and Stew

Of course, we objected to being left alone with Angus Flint. Dad said that it was fair shares because they had him all evening. My mother had the cheek to say to us, "Well, darlings, if you three can't get rid of him, nobody can."

I raved at her. She didn't know what it was like. He took Pip's football away because he said we were making a noise with it. He took all the mouth organs, and Tony's trains. Tony has a way of leaving half-made models about, and Angus Flint used to take them apart whenever he came across them. He said they were in the way. When I went to complain, he was standing on his head.

He always stood on his head after he'd done anything like that. He stood on his head after he stole my paper.

All I'd done was to make a bad drawing of Angus Flint standing on his head. He'd no business to look at my private paper anyway. I drew it because I was so mad at the way Angus Flint would keep insulting the furniture. The boys can stick up for themselves, but Cora's bed can't. Angus Flint said it was lumpy and hard. He told the dining table it was rickety and the chairs they were only fit for scrap. He said the sitting room furniture ought to be burned.

Tony said that if he hated our furniture so much, he should leave. He got the Stare. Pip asked Angus Flint every day when he was going, but he only got the Stare, too. I knew it was no good telling Angus Flint to stop insulting the furniture, so whenever he complained, I said, "That's a very profound idea." And got the Stare.

After that, the boys went around calling everything "very profound," from the curtains to our comics. Angus Flint must have felt they had something. All our comics suddenly disappeared. After searching everywhere else, we found them in Cora's room, where Angus Flint had been reading them. I rushed at Angus Flint to complain, and there he was, standing on his head again, maroon socks waving, and his face, squashed and purple, giving me the Stare upside down at floor level.

"Go away. I've got to do this for five more minutes."

"It looks very profound," I said, but I went away

quickly while I was saying it. By that time I was scared of being picked up by my hair again.

I got picked up by my hair for rescuing Menace. Menace did not appear very often for fear of being patted by Angus Flint. He lurked nervously under cupboards. But one morning he rashly lay down outside the boys' room. Pip and Tony decided that Menace would be able to slide into hiding more easily if he had one of my old roller skates strapped to his middle.

Menace hated the idea.

I heard him hating it and came to help. There was a lot of shouting and a good deal more yelping from Menace. Then Angus Flint came pelting out of Cora's room, roaring at us to be quiet.

Menace fled. He never let Angus Flint get within a foot of him if he could help it. But the skate stayed.

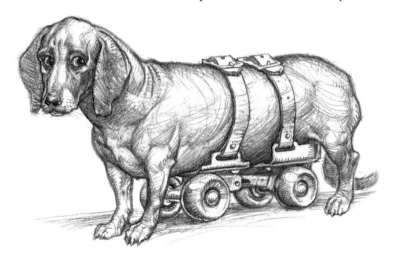

Angus Flint trod on it and shot off downstairs. It was beautiful. We were all sorry when he stopped on the first landing. Then he came pounding upstairs again, shouting, "Whose skate was that?"

I said, "Mine," without thinking.

I was picked up and swung about by my hair. It must have hurt me more than Pip because I'm heavier.

Still, that put an idea into my sore head. I went and borrowed roller skates from everyone I knew. I got armfuls. Pip and Tony helped me bring them home in carrier bags. There we laid them out, the way you do mouse poison, in cunning corners. It was an awful nuisance. Kids kept coming to the door saying, "My sister says she lent you my roller skates, and she's no right to do that because they're mine." But there were quite a few left, even after that.

The result: Pip fell over once, Tony twice, and me three times. Mum and Dad were immune. They said they'd had years of practice. And Angus Flint never said whether he'd fallen over or not. He simply collected all the skates up and threw them in the dustbin. He did it just before the dustmen called, so they were gone before we realized. And kids still keep coming to the door to ask for their skates. I've had to part with most of my nicest things in return.

Tony got picked up by his hair because of the plastic

stew. He wanted revenge because Angus Flint kept breaking his models. And Tony hated the way Angus Flint always took one rabbit nibble at his food and then sounded so surprised that it was nice. Tony got as annoyed over that as I did at the way Angus Flint kept insulting the furniture. Mum was furious, too. After the third time Angus Flint did it, she took to saying pleasantly, "Arsenic does taste nice." At which Angus Flint always gave the same loud, jolly laugh. So I think Mum and Tony put their heads together over the stew.

No we didn't.

Mum just pretended not to see.

Tony.

I'm writing this, not you, Tony Robbins. And you said I could have your paper.

As I was saying, it was stew for supper. Tony had collected all the bits of leftover plastic model he could find. You know the things you have left after you've made a model. They look like knobby fish bones. Tony had collected them from everywhere he could think of. Because most of them came from the floor or the backs of cupboards, there was a good deal of grit and fluff and

Menace's hairs with them, too. Mum put the first spoon-ful of stew on Angus Flint's plate, and while she was dipping for the second spoonful, Tony dumped a great handful of mixed plastic and fluff on top of it. Mum never turned a hair. She just poured orange gravy over the lot and passed it to Angus Flint.

We all watched breathlessly while he took up a forkful and did his nibble. "This—" he began as usual. Then he found what it was. He spat it out. "Who did this?" he said. He knew it was Tony by instinct. He answered his own question by picking Tony up by his hair and carrying him out of the room.

Mum knocked over her chair and rushed out after them. But by the time we all got to the hall—we got in one another's way a little—Tony was upstairs running his head under the cold tap. And Angus Flint was—yes, you guessed it!—upside down on the hall carpet.

"I don't want any supper, Margaret," his squashed face said.

Mum said, "Good!" to the maroon socks and stormed back to the dining room.

4

Cream Teas

Next morning there was nothing for breakfast. Angus Flint had got up in the night and eaten all the cornflakes and all the milk, and fried himself all the eggs.

"Why is there no food?" he demanded.

"You ate it all," Mum said.

Angus Flint did not seem to notice how cold she sounded. He just set to work to eat all the bread and marmalade, too. He simply did not see how we all hated him. He really enjoyed staying with us. He kept saying so. Every evening when my parents crawled home to him, he would meet them with a beaming smile. "This is such a friendly household, Margaret," he said. "You've done me a lot of good."

"I think we must be very profound," Pip said drearily.

"I suppose I couldn't live here always?" said Angus Flint.

There was silence. A very profound one.

Pip broke the silence by stumping off to do his practice. By that time the only time either of us dared practice was when our parents were at home. Angus Flint would not let us touch the piano. If you started, he came and picked you up by your hair. Pip and I got so that we used to dive off the stool and under the piano as soon as we heard a footstep. Pip's True Love, when he did manage to play her, seemed to have developed a squint as well as a stutter, and as for my gloomy elephants, they had got more like despairing dinosaurs. I kept having to apologize to the piano—not to speak of Miss Hawksmoore.

"You should sell that piano," Angus Flint said as Pip started bashing away.

Mum would not hear of it. The piano is her best bargain ever. Not everyone can buy a perfect concert grand for £10. Besides, she wanted us to learn to play it.

By this time Angus Flint had stayed with us for nearly a fortnight. Cora was due home in three days, and he still showed no signs of leaving. The boys told him he would have to leave when Cora came back, but all they got was the Stare. My parents both realized that something would have to be done and began to show a little firmness at last. Mum explained—in her special anxious way that she uses when she doesn't want to offend someone—that Cora was coming back soon and would need her room. Dad took to starting everything he said to Angus Flint with "When you leave us—" But Angus Flint took not the slightest bit of notice. It began to dawn on me that he really did intend to stay for good.

I was soon sure of it. He suddenly went all charming. He left me some breakfast for once. He even made his bed, and he was polite all morning. I warned the boys, but they wouldn't believe me. I warned Mum, too, when she came back suddenly in the middle of the afternoon, but it was a hot day, and she was too tired to listen.

"I only keep buying things if I stay out," she said. "I'd rather face Angus Flint than the bank manager."

Too right, she kept buying things. That week she'd bought two hideous three-legged tables for the sitting room, about eight bookcases, and four rolled-up carpets. We were beginning to look like an old furniture store.

Angus Flint heard Mum come back. He rushed up to her with a jolly smile on his face. "Isn't it a lovely day, Margaret? What do you say to me taking you and the kids out to tea somewhere?"

Mum agreed like a shot. He hadn't paid for a thing up to then. The boys had visions of ice cream and cream buns. I knew there was a catch in it, but it was just the day for tea out on a lawn somewhere, and I did feel we ought at least to get that out of Angus Flint in return for all our suffering. So we all crammed into his car.

Angus Flint drove exactly the way you might expect, far too fast. He honked his horn a lot, overtook everything he could—particularly on corners—and he expected old ladies to leap like deer in order not to be run over. Mum said what about the Copper Kettle? Tony said the cakes in the other place were better. But Angus Flint insisted that he had seen "a perfect little place," on his way to stay with us.

We drove three times around town looking for the perfect little place, at top speed. Our name was mud in every street by then. We called out whenever we saw a café of any kind after a while, but Angus Flint just said, "We can't stop here," and sped on.

After nearly an hour, when Pip was near despair, we ended up roaring through Palham, which is a village about three miles out of town. There was a Tea Shoppe with striped umbrellas. Our spirit was broken by then. We didn't even mention it. But Angus Flint stopped with a screech of brakes. "This looks as if it might do," he said.

We all piled out and sat under an umbrella.

"Well, what will you have?" said Angus Flint.

Deep breaths were drawn, and cream teas for five were ordered. We all waited, looking forward to cream and cakes. We felt we really deserved our teas.

Angus Flint said, "I've applied for a job in your town, Margaret. The interview's tomorrow. Your husband was good enough to say that I could make my home with you. Don't you think that's a good idea?"

We stared. Had Dad said that?

"There's Cora," Mum said. "We've no room."

"That's no problem," Angus Flint said. "You can put the two girls in together."

"No!" I said. If you knew Cora—!

"I'd pay," Angus Flint said, joking and trying to be nice. "A nominal sum—a pound a month, say?"

Mum drew herself up resolutely, to my great relief. "No, Angus. It's absolutely out of the question. You'll have to go as soon as Cora comes back."

Angus Flint did not answer. Instead he bounced jovially to his feet. "I have to go and see someone for a moment," he said. "I shan't be long. Don't wait for me." And he was back in his car and driving away before any of us could move.

5

Angus flint's Revenge

They brought us five cream teas almost at once. It was a perfect revenge.

Mum could not believe that Angus Flint was not coming back. We ate our cream teas. After a while Mum let the boys eat Angus's cream tea, too, and said we could order another when he came back. When they came with the bill, she said we were expecting a friend, who would pay.

Half an hour later they began to look at us oddly.

Half an hour after that they took the umbrellas out of the tables and stood the chairs on them suggestively.

A short while after that they came and asked to be paid. They made it quite clear that they knew we were trying to cheat them. They refused Mum's desperately offered check. We had to go through all our pockets and shake Mum's bag out on the table, and even then we were two pennies short. They forgave us that, but grimly. They looked after us unlovingly as we went. Mum nearly sank under the embarrassment.

Then we had to walk home. It was still hot. Tony hates walking, and he whined. Pip got a blister and whined, too. Mum snarled, and I snapped. We were all in the worst tempers of our lives by the time we plunged up the garden path and burst into the house. We knew that Angus Flint would be standing there, upside down on the hall carpet, to meet us.

"And this time I shan't care that it's his socks I'm talking to!" I said.

But the person standing in the hall was Dad. He was the right way up, of course, and wondering where we'd all got to. Mum went for him with both fangs out. "Have you had the nerve to tell Angus Flint that he could live with us? If so—" I felt quite sorry for my father. He admitted that in the heat of the first reunion, he might have said some such thing, but— Oh, boy! Never have I heard my mother give tongue the way she did then. I couldn't do it half so well. Even Cora couldn't, the time she acted King Herod at school.

After that, for a beautiful, peaceful half evening, we thought Angus Flint had gone for good. We kept the window shut, played the piano, watched the things we wanted on the telly, and cheered Dad up by playing cards with him. We were all thoroughly happy when Angus Flint came back again. He knew we were likely to complain, I suppose, so he brought a girlfriend home with him to make sure we couldn't go for him.

The girlfriend was a complete stranger to us. Handpicked for idiocy, with glasses and a giggle.

"Teach her to play cards," said Angus Flint. "She's quite clever really."

She wasn't. But neither was Angus Flint when it came to cards. Have you ever played cards with somebody who thinks for twenty minutes before he puts a card down and then puts down exactly the wrong one? He played the girl's hand, too, though she was slightly better at it than he was. We went to bed after the first game. But Angus Flint didn't take the girlfriend home until well after midnight. I know, because I heard Mum let fly again when he did.

Angus Flint came back at three and woke me up hammering at the front door.

When I let him in, he said, "Didn't you hear me knocking? I might have caught my death."

I said, "I wish you had!" and escaped into the sitting room before he could pick me up by my hair.

Menace was there. He crawled nervously out from under the piano to be stroked.

"Menace," I said. "Where's your spirit? Can't you bite Angus Flint?"

Then I thought that I didn't dare bite Angus Flint either, and got so miserable that I went wandering around the room. I patted the uncomfortable chairs and the poor ugly tables and stroked the piano.

"Chairs," I said, "stand up for yourselves! He insults you all the time. Tables," I said, "he said you ought to be burned! Piano, he told Mum to sell you. Do something, all of you! Furniture of the world, unite!" I made them a very stirring speech, all about the rights of oppressed furniture, and it made me feel much better. Not that I thought it would do any good. But I thought it was a very good idea.

6

The Tables Turn

Next morning Angus Flint ate my breakfast as usual, and Mum and Dad went out together to make friends again. Leaving us alone with Angus Flint, yet again!

At least there was something "very profound" on the telly that afternoon. First I ever knew that racehorses were profound, but it meant twenty minutes' peace. I did some practice. The piano sounded lovely. My elfin elephants shrank in size and were beginning to sound like mere hobnailed goblins when the door was torn open. I knew it was Angus Flint and dived for safety.

He was in a very bad temper. I think his horse lost. As I crawled out from under the piano, he sat down at it, grumbling, and started to hammer out a sonata. I was surprised to see that he knew how to play. But he played very badly. Menace began to whine under his cupboard.

Angus Flint thumped both hands down with a jangle. "This is a horrible piano," he said. "It's got a terrible tone, and it needs tuning."

Rotten slander. I don't blame the piano for getting annoyed. Its curved black rear shuddered. One of its stumpy front legs pawed the ground. Then its lid shut with a clap on Angus Flint's fingers. Now I know why Mum got it for only £10. Angus Flint dragged his fingers free with such a yell that Pip and Tony came to see what was happening.

By the time they got there, both the new ugly little tables were stealing toward Angus Flint for a surprise attack, each with its three legs twinkling cautiously over the carpet. Angus Flint saw one out of the corner of his eye and turned to Stare at it. It stood where it was, looking innocent. But the piano stool spun itself around and tipped him on the floor. I think that was very loyal of the stool, because it must have been the one piece of furniture Angus Flint had not insulted. And while Angus Flint was sprawling on the floor, the best chair trundled up and did its best to run him over. He scrambled out of its way with a howl. And the nearest bookcase promptly showered him with books. While he was trying to get up, the piano lowered its music stand and charged.

I don't blame Angus Flint for being terrified. The

piano was gnashing its keys at him and kicking out with its pedals and snorting through the holes in its music stand. And it went galloping around the room after Angus Flint on its three brass casters like a mad black bull. The rest of the furniture kept blundering across his path. Tables knocked him this way and that, and chairs herded him into huddles of other chairs. But they always left him a free way to run when the piano charged, so that he had a thoroughly frightening time. They never once tried to hurt the three of us.

I stuffed myself into a corner and admired. That piano was an expert. It would come thundering down on Angus Flint. When he tore off frantically sideways, it stopped short and banged its lid down within inches of his trouser seat. It could turn in its own length and be after him again before you could believe it to be possible. Angus Flint dashed around and around the sitting room, and the piano thundered after him, and when the boys had to leave the doorway, one of the new bookcases dodged over and stood across it, so that Angus Flint was utterly trapped.

"Do something, can't you!" he kept howling at me, and I only laughed.

The reason the boys had to leave the doorway was that the dining room table had heard the fun going on and wanted to join in. The trouble was, both its rickety wings were spread out and it was too wide to get through the dining room door. It was in the doorway, clattering its feet and banging furiously for help. Tony and Pip took pity on it and took its wings down. It then scuttled across the hall, nudged aside the bookcase, and dived into the sitting room after Angus Flint, flapping both wings like a great angry bird. And it wasn't going to play cat and mouse like the piano. It was out to get Angus Flint. He had some very narrow escapes and howled louder than ever.

I thought the time had come to widen the scene a little. I made my way around the walls, with tables and chairs trundling this way and that all around me, and opened the window.

Angus Flint howled out that I was a good girl—which annoyed me—and made for the opening like a bat out of hell. I meant to trip him when he got there. I didn't want him getting too much of a start. But the carpet saved me the trouble by flipping up one of its corners around his feet. He came down on his face, half inside the room and half in the garden. The piano and the dining table both bore down on him. He scrambled up and bolted. I've never seen anyone run so fast.

The table was after him like a shot, but the piano got its rear caster stuck on the sill. It must be very awkward having to gallop with only one leg at the back. I went to help it, but the faithful piano stool and my favorite chair got there first and heaved it free. Then it hunched its wide front part and fairly shot across the garden and out into the road after the flying Angus Flint. The chairs and tables all set out, too, bravely bobbling and trundling. Last of all went Menace, barking as if he were doing all the chasing single-handed.

I don't know what the other people in the street thought. The dining table collided with a lamppost halfway down the street and put itself out of the running. But the piano got up speed wonderfully and was hard on Angus Flint's heels as he shot into the next street. After that we lost them. We were too busy collecting exhausted tables and chairs, which were strewn all down the street.

The piano stool had only got as far as the garden gate, and my favorite chair broke a caster getting through the window. We had to carry them back to the house. And there was a fair amount of tidying up to do indoors, what with the books, the carpets, and Cora's bed.

Cora's bed, probably the most insulted piece of furniture in the house, must have been frantic to get at Angus Flint, too. It had forced itself halfway through the bedroom door and then stuck. We had a terrible job getting it back inside the room. We had just done it and were wearily trying to mend the dining table—which has never been the same since—when we heard twanging and clattering noises coming from the sitting room. We were in time to see the piano come plodding back through the window and put itself in its usual place. It looked tired but satisfied.

"Do you think it's eaten him?" Pip said hopefully.

The piano didn't say. But it hadn't. Mum and Dad came back, and we were all cheerfully having a cup of tea when Angus Flint suddenly came shooting downstairs. We think he climbed up the drainpipe in order not to meet the piano again. I suspect that Cora's bed was rather glad to see him.

"I'm just leaving," Angus Flint said.

It was music to our ears! He went straight out to his car, too, carrying his suitcase. We all came out to say polite good-bye—or polite good-riddance, as Tony put it.

"I've had a wonderful time," Angus Flint said. "Here's a football for you, Pip." And he held out to Pip a flat orange thing. It was Pip's own football, but it was burst. "And this is for you," he said to Tony, handing him a fistful of broken plastic. Then he said to me, "I'm giving you some paper." And he gave me one sheet of my own paper. One sheet! I'd had a whole new block.

"I do hope Cora's bed bit you," I said sweetly.

Angus Flint gave me the Stare for that, but it wasn't as convincing as usual, somehow. Then he got into his car and drove away. Actually drove away and didn't come back. We cheered.

It's been so peaceful since. Mum wondered whether to sell the new tables, but we wouldn't let her. They are our faithful friends. As for the piano, well, Pip has decided he's going to be a genius at something else instead. His excuse for giving up lessons is that Miss Hawksmoore's false teeth make her spit on his hands when she's teaching him. They do. But the real reason is that he's scared of the piano. I'm not. I love it more than that coward Menace, even, and I'm determined to work and work until I've learned how to play it as it deserves.